From the shadows of the grass
HIROSHIMA

D1736277

Hiroshima – From the shadows of the grass

Author & Publisher: Toshinori Kanaya

© TOSHINORI KANAYA 2015
Published August 7, 2015.

Translator: Geoffrey Trousselot
Cover Design: Takeshi Nagamatsu
Editing Assistance: Osamu Yamazaki (Yuyusha)
Data Creation Supervisor: ePublishing LAB.

This book is the English translation of the electronic edition of the original book in Japanese (ISBN978-4-7790-1106-1), which was first published in 2014 by Gentosha Renaissance Inc. (currently Gentosha Media Consulting Inc.).

Table of Contents

Prologue ··7

Chapter 1: Early Childhood ·································17

Chapter 2: Hiroshima First Middle School ·······················37

Chapter 3: Little Boy ···81

Chapter 4: August 6, 1945, Hiroshima ························ 101

Chapter 5: Reminiscence ································· 121

Epilogue ······································· 143

Afterword ·································· 161

Bibliography ·································· 165

Map of Hiroshima City before the Atomic Bomb
Provided by Ed. Shinkosha "Nippon Chiri Fuzoku Taikei (Japanese Geography and Culture)"

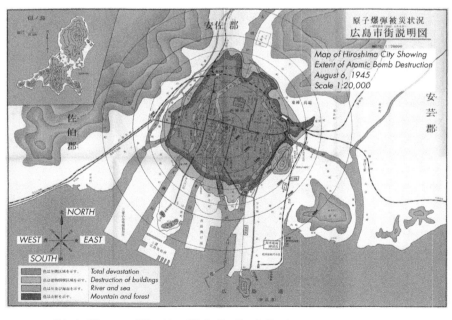

Extent of Damage of Hiroshima City by the Atomic Bomb
(Record of the Hiroshima A-bomb War Disaster. Appendix I. Hiroshima City. 1971.)
Provided by Hiroshima City

Notes

Prologue

Hiroshima is a city surrounded by rivers. It was created on a triangular shaped delta that spreads out wide at the river mouth where Ota River runs into Hiroshima Bay. Nowadays, there are six distributaries that flow through the city in a branch formation. If you walk around a little in the city, in no time you will come to a bank of one of the tributaries. In fact, the many people coming into and out of this city necessarily have to cross multiple bridges along their way. Hiroshima is that sort of city. It is even sometimes called "the City of Water."

Over the tributary Kyobashi River from Hiroshima's city center, at 4-60 Deshio-cho 2-chome, Minami Ward, stands a complex of buildings called the Hiroshima Army Clothing Depot. These brick buildings, looking like gigantic warehouses, are one of the so-called A-bombed buildings. Before the war, the depot was used for manufacturing and storing the clothing standard of the Japanese Army. The still-standing No. 10 to 13 warehouses were constructed in 1913.

This out-of-place building exterior is a section of the landscape that is alien from the surrounding modern-day urban buildings and the din of cars passing down nearby roads. The buildings seem to reside in an eerie silence, alone in another dimension of space. Such is the impression imprinted in visitors' minds.

On August 6, 1945, these buildings were left structurally intact by the immense impact of the atomic bomb dropped on Hiroshima. Although the steel shutters covering the windows on the west side, facing ground zero, were bent inwards by the impact of the blast wave, the other parts of the buildings were well retained partly due to the 2.7-kilometer distance from ground zero and partly due to its solid architecture. And so, for the nearly 70 years that have passed until today, the buildings stand as if nothing happened. The depot's state of abandonment, however, is obvious from the weeds that grow around it. This feeling of deadness is somehow further enhanced by the youthful lively chatter coming from the students exercising on the nearby high-school grounds.

On August 6, 1945, due to the dropping of the atomic bomb on this city, my uncle Yoshio Kanaya died in a corner of this building, away from his family. He was 15.

Directly after the bomb was dropped, just like all the emergency refuges in Hiroshima on that day, this depot was like hell on earth. Unknown numbers of victims had evacuated there in swarms from Hiroshima's center. Many of these people, one after the other, breathed their last. And with such a high death toll, there was no possible way to respectfully attend to the dead. The only evidence that my uncle had died is his listing in an atomic bombing fatality register, "Yoshio Kanaya. Died August 7, 1945. Aged 15 years. Army Clothing Depot." Neither his remains, nor any article left by him, were passed on to our family.

The first time I had the faintest idea that I had an uncle who died in the atomic bombing was when I was in the junior section of elementary school. At the time, I lived in a family of five, comprising myself, my parents, my grandfather, and my younger sister. Except for me and my sister, who were born after the war, my parents and my grandfather were A-bomb survivors. This made me and my sister second generation A-bomb survivors.

My grandfather was still healthy back then, and every August 6, "A-Bomb Day," it was a decided routine that he would take me and my sister from our house in the western suburbs of Hiroshima to the city

Entrance of the Army Clothing Depot
Provided by Toshinori Kanaya

Courtyard of the Army Clothing Depot
Provided by Toshinori Kanaya

center.

When we arrived in the city center, we first paid a visit to the memorial monument located in the Peace Park. Then, every year in the evening, as the sun was beginning to set, we went to the stepped pier of the Motoyasu River where we placed floating lanterns in the river to send off the spirits of the fallen atomic bomb victims. I was still in the junior section of elementary school, and didn't understand the full significance of A-Bomb Day on August 6. But I was happy that my grandfather brought us into the city and I always eagerly looked forward to August 6. But when I went to the floating lanterns, in a naïve kind of way, my heart somehow sunk.

Then, when I was in the senior section of elementary school, at the place of the floating lanterns, my grandfather handed me a lantern and got me to write the name "Yoshio" on it.

"Your uncle."

That was all that my grandfather said. And having always been an introspective type of person myself, I did not venture to ask my grandfather about the kind of life this person called Yoshio led.

I simply watched the lantern with the name "Yoshio," which I had clumsily written in black ink, drift along the dark river surface, moving slowly away from the moored flat-bottom boats at the pier, while the chanting of sutra bellowed from a PA system. By then the sun had well and truly set, and the multicolored candle-lit floating lanterns all drifted off in the same direction, swaying to and fro over the dark river surface.

The floating lanterns drifted across the river surface in various ways. There were lanterns that drifted along in solitary loneliness, clusters of lanterns that seemed to have been drawn to each other, and among these, there were also lanterns no longer drifting anywhere as they had become stuck in the river mud. Looking at the glowing, floating lanterns aimlessly drifting over the dark river surface, I felt a deep sorrow in my young heart, which overshadowed my appreciation of the fantastic beauty.

Intermingling with each other, the countless floating lanterns drifted across the river surface. While it was riding the flow and drifting far away, the lantern that I had written "Yoshio" on had merged with other lanterns, and at some point or other it become impossible to tell one from the other. That moment always reminded me that I would never, in all eternity, meet the person called Yoshio who had passed away before I came into existence, and that made me sad. This became a growing up experience for me, repeated every year on August 6 throughout my childhood.

Then, when I was in my mid-teens, my grandfather reached an age when he no longer went out, and we stopped going to the floating lanterns. However, every year on the morning of August 6, it was still the family custom to sit together in silence at 8:15 a.m., the time the atomic bomb exploded on Hiroshima. For A-bomb survivors and their families, August 6 was a day with special significance. For our family, in addition to it being a day for paying tribute to the people who died in the atomic bombing, it was also the day to remember Uncle Yoshio.

The way I saw my uncle back then, however, was simply this person whose memory I invoked just once a year on A-Bomb Day. I was only putting my hands in prayer in the same way as the rest of my family, and I didn't have deep emotions for my uncle. Inside my head, my uncle only existed in the abstract. He was someone I had never met whose face I never knew. For me, even though he was my uncle, it seemed only natural that I couldn't feel much emotion while paying tribute to the memory of a person whose face I could not picture.

Neither my grandfather nor my parents were inclined to talk about the atomic bomb being dropped on Hiroshima, let alone anything about my uncle. This was especially so when I was a child, but it was even the case after I had grown up. Being just as incommunicative as the rest of the family, I didn't press to ask about it either. And so, I spent my days in a state of not knowing even the smallest detail about my family's experience as A-bomb survivors. I knew hardly anything about the dropping of the bomb apart from, say, stories of A-bomb survivors I had learned from the media and books. Although I was a second-generation A-bomb survivor, my feelings toward the atomic bomb were simply the vague emotions I felt from what general knowledge I had.

That is not to say that I didn't understand why my family and many other A-bomb survivors didn't talk of their own experiences of the bombing. Many people living in Hiroshima on August 6, 1945, experienced traumatic horrors from the atomic bombing. Over 100,000 people died within the space of three months. The people who experienced and survived the bombing carried indescribably deep mental and physical scars. Many are continuing to suffer the aftereffects, even today. It is only natural that these people do not talk about their harrowing past.

On the other hand, my family could probably be described as the fortunate survivors. While my whole family, excluding myself and my younger sister, were A-bomb survivors, no one suffered any severe atom-bomb related illness, and including my relatives, the only person in our family to have perished in the bombing was my uncle.

Among the citizens of Hiroshima, there were many cases of entire families dying due to the atomic bomb, and it was not uncommon for children who escaped the bombing owing to the evacuation of school children to ironically become orphans through the deaths of all other members of their families, who were in the city center. Then there are many people who have continually suffered long-standing aftereffects from the bombing. From the perspective of the related parties of these A-bomb victims, our family could be seen as a fortunate A-bomb survivor family. Nonetheless, the death of my uncle at age 15 from the atomic bomb was a tragedy amid such fortune.

My uncle was in third grade at middle school when the bomb hit. The Hiroshima Prefectural Hiroshima First Middle School at which he was attending was about 900 meters from ground zero. Because the teachers and students at the school had mostly either died instantly or suffered mortal injuries, it was naturally assumed that my uncle, who was in the school on that day, had died on August 6 at the school. As was the case for many of the students who died at the school, my uncle's remains were never found. Left in the uncertainty that he probably died somewhere at the school, my family naturally assumed that my uncle's final day was August 6.

It was not until August 2, 1973, nearly 30 years after the bombing, that I discovered my uncle's actual date and place of death. I was a 22-year-old university student at the time. Every year from August 1, atomic bomb fatality registers for unidentified victims were on public display at the Hiroshima Peace Memorial Museum located in the Peace Park. On that day, I had gone alone to visit the museum. I cannot recall my reason for going now, but I suspect I probably had a feeling I would find my uncle's name there. The registers on public display were sorted according to the local police station whose jurisdictional area contained the facility where the victims had died. Then I saw my uncle's name in the register of victims that died inside the jurisdictional area of Ujina Police Station. For a moment, I was overcome by a delusion that I was meeting my uncle. While gazing at my uncle's name written on the register, the name gradually became blurry as my tears swelled.

"Yoshio Kanaya. Died August 7, 1945. Aged 15 years. Army Clothing Depot."

I realized that my uncle, after suffering the blast, had somehow, either by struggling on his own strength or by being carried, managed to get to the Army Clothing Depot, some 1.6 kilometers from the school. Moreover, he had stayed alive for close to a day.

I think that the reason my grandfather and father had not gone and looked at all the fatality registers was because they never doubted that my uncle had died at the middle school on August 6. After finding out my uncle's date of death, my family, while continuing to practice the silent prayer on August 6, began to pray for my uncle's soul on August 7. But still, although we know the place and date of his death, his remains, and any articles that were with him on that day, are forever lost.

Over this time, both my grandfather and father had passed away, and gone forever was any opportunity to ask the close relatives with whom my uncle had shared his life to tell me about my uncle who lived and died before me. Then, my feelings toward my uncle once again, little by little, began fading away. However, one day, I found an unfamiliar item among the mementos of my father.

At the beginning of 1945, directly before the atomic bombing, my grandfather feared that Hiroshima would soon also be the target of a large-scale air raid by the U.S. Military. He had moved precious items from Yokogawa-cho (now Yokogawa-cho, Nishi Ward, Hiroshima) to Midorii Village (now Midorii, Asaminami Ward, Hiroshima). Thanks to this decision, quite a collection of documents and the like, including photos and negatives taken by my father as one of his hobbies before the war, escaped destruction by the atomic bombing. My grandfather had continued to safeguard them carefully even after the war. Among this collection were photos of my uncle and documents my uncle had written. All letters addressed to my uncle throughout 1945 that were sent to the family home in Yokogawa were destroyed by the atomic bomb. The letters that my uncle had written and sent to people outside Hiroshima had escaped the bombing and fortunately remained. After the war, these letters were returned to my grandfather.

For the first time, I looked upon the features of my uncle, who appeared in several of the photos. I marveled at how the face of that teenager in the photos resembled me in my teenage years. Like two peas in a pod you could say. That face looked more like me as a teenager than my father's face when he was that age. For a moment, the notion of reincarnation even passed through my mind.

I then read the letters written by my uncle over and over again. They were spirited and carefree sentences written in the style of a teenage boy.

Until I had cast my eyes on the mementos of my father, the idea I had formed of my uncle was vague and detached. However, for the first time, feelings inside wanted to embrace my uncle as a close relative. These feelings rose irrepressibly, making me really want to know about this teenage boy called Yoshio, whom I had never met. What was the life he lived, and how did he pass from this world? In dedication to my uncle, I decided to write about his short life to preserve it in writing, and construct a tombstone for my uncle by my own pen.

Notes

Chapter 1: Early Childhood

Yoshio was born the fourth son of Kiyosuke, his father, and Futayo, his mother, on February 5, 1930. The first-born son was Seiji, my father, the second-born son was Hiroshi, and the third-born son was Takao. It was a family of all boys.

When Yoshio was born, Kiyosuke was 40 and Futayo was 34. At the time, Seiji was 10, Hiroshi was 8, and Takao was 6. Yoshio was ten years younger than his eldest brother Seiji.

Kiyosuke ran a company called Kansai Manmade Fertilizer Co., Ltd. It manufactured and sold mainly chemical fertilizer in Misasa-cho. The business was founded in August 1913 as Hiroshima Manufacturing Manure and Cotton, Co., Ltd.

The entire neighborhood of Misasa-cho was already called the trading district of Hiroshima by 1907. It was a busy town containing many factories. Besides manufacturing manmade fertilizer, the town also manufactured timber, indigo dyes, needles, brushes, soap, raw silk, among others. Of these, the needle manufacturing was one of the best in Japan, and in 1919 there were as many as 29 factories in Misasa-cho. In 1910, a railway line called Hiroshima Electric Railway (now JR Kabe Line) was opened. It ran between Yokogawa-cho, which was then a part of Misasa-cho, and Kabe (Kabe, Asakita Ward, Hiroshima). Trade also flourished through river transportation on the Ota River. As a result, Misasa-cho became the sole town that received all incoming freight from the northern part of Hiroshima Prefecture.

In the proximity of Kansai Manmade Fertilizer Co., Ltd., several warehouses for these factories were built. Materials that had been carted down Ota River were off-loaded onto broad stone steps several tens of meters wide called the Ogangi Pier. It was there, just at the top of these stairs, that the Kansai Manmade Fertilizer warehouse was built. Part of the Ogangi Pier that existed at that time is still exists today as a historical landmark.

The family home was in Yokogawa-cho, a short walk from the

company. The house was built on a river bank not far from a junction of three rivers, where Ota River branches into Hon River and Tenma River. Viewing the river from the house, you could see Ota River flowing seaward and branching into two tributaries on the left, Hon River located roughly straight south, and Tenma River flowing seaward on the right.

As the house was built on the river embankment with the river flowing directly below, it was possible to cast fishing lines and catch fish from inside the house. A boat was moored to the riverbank directly below the house, and in the spring and summer, the family would take it out boating.

When Yoshio was born, in addition to his parents and three brothers, his family also included Tomotaro, his grandfather, and Masa, his grandmother. Kiyosuke had been adopted. Futayo had moved from Itsukaichi-cho (now Yahata, Saeki Ward, Hiroshima) to be Kiyosuke's bride. So practically speaking for Tomotaro and Masa, this was an adoption of a successor and his bride.

Since always, Grandfather Tomotaro was a frequent philanderer. Behind Masa's back, he would be often sneaking off to the pleasure quarters and cavorting with geishas. One day, Tomotaro decided he would take his grandson Seiji to a restaurant. Seeing the two of them heading off, Masa asked where they were going.

"And where would you two be going?"

She asked.

"I'm just going out for a stroll with Seiji."

Tomotaro replied with a face of pure innocence.

When they arrived at the restaurant, Tomotaro went off to do what he really came for. Meanwhile, left alone in a different room, Seiji found himself spoiled by geishas for whom the presence of a young child was a rare sight. There, he was treated to an omelet.

When Tomotaro and Seiji came home, Masa asked Seiji in a sweet voice.

"Where did you go with Grandpa?"

Seiji just looked down at the floor silently, and Masa saw right through the charade.

For a while, Tomotaro continued working and living his carefree lifestyle. However, he eventually got fed up with the cramped home life, or something or other, and handed down the business to Kiyosuke. After doing that, he moved out of the house alone to go and live with a mistress at another house in Rakurakuen located in the western suburbs (now Rakurakuen, Saeki Ward, Hiroshima), where he led a life of retirement. Naturally this caused a chill in Tomotaro and Masa's relationship. Most likely due to this household environment, Masa ignored Futayo and monopolized her first grandson Seiji, apparently completely doting on him.

Kiyosuke was a man with a straight-laced and methodical personality. After Tomotaro had entrusted him with looking after the company and the family, he became the sort of man who took stern control of the household in the style of a typical Meiji-period-born patriarch. Nevertheless, he was also a family-oriented man who held feelings for his family. It was his nature to be a stickler for details, and no one could have been more passionate about the children's education than he was.

Futayo was a quiet and calm woman. Like Kiyosuke, she was brought up in the Meiji period, and accordingly, she did not act ahead of her husband. However, there was more to her than just her reserved persona. Although she did not assert herself, she was still an intellectual woman.

There was just once when Futayo took assertive action. On that occasion, Kiyosuke had become intimate with a certain geisha. Completely unforgiving of her husband's actions, Futayo left the house and returned to her family home. Her parents told her that Kiyosuke was a good provider and that she should endure. In a tearful state, Futayo was sent back to the Yokogawa-cho home. Futayo, acting as if nothing had happened, devoted herself to the home.

Futayo was masterful at dealing with slightly frictional family relations in the house. The family environment was quite typical for that day and age. Nevertheless, as the family was a large one, with a mother-in-law in addition to her husband, and four children, daily household chores were endless. Due to her husband's work, she also had to worry herself about entertaining businessmen who came and went. Even so, she was never known to complain. A particular tension was how her mother-in-law Masa doted over Seiji and never left his side. It created a relationship where Futayo, who was Seiji's mother, was unable to have a say in Seiji's upbringing. However, as Futayo was a reasonable woman, rather than allowing her discontent to leak out, she showed indifference and devoted herself to the daily household chores. Masa also showed tolerance toward Futayo with all things other than Seiji's upbringing, and so the relationship between mother-in-law and daughter-in-law was, on the whole, not a bad one.

Among Yoshio's brothers, Seiji the eldest was a bright and well-behaved child right from early childhood. After entering elementary school, he performed well academically and was the class monitor throughout the six years. The second eldest Hiroshi was bright like Seiji, and he was well behaved as well. However ever since birth, he had a weak constitution and often raised a fever. Takao, Yoshio's nearest-elder brother, also lacked physical strength. Takao died prematurely aged only 8.

Incidentally, the place the family home was on was government land. Nowadays, the land is zoned as a green belt zone of a river bank. Looking south from there, one can look directly down the Hon River, and the Atomic Bomb Dome can be seen standing in the distance. Due to this geographical relationship, the family home took the full brunt of destructive force from the atomic bomb that was dropped on August 6, 1945. Specifically, the place where the family home was is about 1 kilometer north of ground zero. As the south of the house faced the river, the immeasurably powerful thermic rays and blast wind hit with full force and the family house collapsed and burned immediately. At the time, Kiyosuke was at the company, which was located close to the family home, and although he was injured, being inside saved him from getting burned, and he narrowly escaped with his life. Moreover, aside from Yoshio, Kiyosuke was the only member of the family living at Yokogawa-cho at the time. Grandfather and grandmother, mother, and Takao were already dead, and Seiji and Hiroshi were saved by being in a different place.

The world into which Yoshio was born was directly before Japan made the entire region from Asia to the Pacific Ocean its battle field and plunged itself into full-scale war with China, the United States, and the other countries. It was truly a year that was ushering in the age when the whole of Japan would walk down a road of suffering, starting in 1931 with the Manchurian Incident and leading to the end of the war in 1945.

In 1930 when Yoshio was born, a wave of recession was beating down on Japanese society. The massive stock price collapse that had begun on Wall Street the year earlier caused financial panic throughout the world, and the effect hit Japan hard. Against the backdrop of this global crisis, there were various incidents, such as the signing of the Treaty for the Limitation and Reduction of Naval Armament, and the attempted assassination of Osachi Hamaguchi by right wing ultranationalists. An air of discontent began drifting through the country. Nevertheless, many people still led their lives not sensing the air of impending war.

However, in 1931, when the Manchurian Incident broke out and the Japanese Kantogun (Kwantung Army) began invading Northeast China, a mood of disquiet spread steadily throughout Japan.

On April 28, 1932, when Yoshio was 2 years old, Takao died at age 8. His cause of death was not entirely clear, but surmising from what my grandfather said and so forth, it was most probably miliary tuberculosis. As Yoshio was only 2 years old when Takao passed away, he probably didn't have any memory of elder brother Takao. You could say from

Yoshio's perspective that he only had two brothers, as there were just Seiji and Hiroshi ever since he was walking and talking.

In the year that Takao died, from February through March, an ultranationalist group led by Nissho Inoue assassinated former Finance Minister Junnosuke Inoue and Director-General of Mitsui Holding Company, Dan Takuma, in what is called the League of Blood Incident. Then, on May 15, Prime Minister Tsuyoshi Inukai was shot dead at the Prime Minister's Residence by young naval officers. Such incidents contributed to an ominous feeling slowly penetrating society. Most of the general public who learned of these incidents didn't fully comprehend the direction in which Japan was then heading, but after witnessing a series of murderous incidents involving the prime minister and core politicians, they began feeling uneasy about these strange happenings. Ignoring such unease among the people, Japan withdrew from the League of Nations in March 1933 in protest of the refusal to recognize Manchukuo. With its back turned to international society, Japan continued its armed invasion of mainland China and began taking the path to full-scale war.

At the time, Hiroshima was called the military capital. What created Hiroshima's image as the military capital stems back as far as the Meiji period. In 1888, the 5th Division was established and the Imperial Japanese Naval Academy was moved from Tokyo to Etajima. In 1889, one of the major naval bases called Headquarters for Pacification and Defense was opened in the city of Kure, and in 1890, the Eastern Parade Ground was established. Then in 1894, during the Sino-Japanese War, the 5th Division and the 11th Infantry Regiment were dispatched from Ujina Port to the Korean Peninsula, and the Western Parade Ground was established. Also in that year, the Sanyo Railway opened a railway line from Mihara to Hiroshima (now JR Sanyo Honsen), and a military railway was constructed from Hiroshima to Ujina. In September of that year, the imperial headquarters was established at Hiroshima Castle. In 1897, a military school for young boys was opened and a naval shipbuilding depot was established at Kure, located south of Hiroshima. In 1904, the Army Clothing Depot was established, and amid the beginning of the Russo-Japanese War, many infantry were dispatched to the continent from Ujina Port. In this way, through its wartime role in both the First Sino-Japanese War and the Russo-Japanese War, Hiroshima became an important base in western Japan for the advancement of armed forces toward the continent. Many military facilities were constructed in the area centered on Hiroshima. Moreover, throughout the First World War and then from the Showa period onward, the military roles of Hiroshima just grew and grew.

In the midst of these disquieting social circumstances, Yoshio's early life carried on. I don't know much detail about his early life except that, in contrast to his two elder brothers, he was an energetic and high-spirited child.

Yoshio as a young boy
Provided by Toshinori Kanaya

In 1936 when Yoshio was 6, an event took place in snow-covered Tokyo that shook the nation. It was the February 26 Incident. On the morning of that day, about 1,400 commissioned officers, noncommissioned officers and soldiers of the 1st Inventory Regiment, the 3rd Imperial Guard, and the 3rd Inventory Regiment attacked Prime Minister Keisuke Okada, Cabinet Minister Makoto Saito, Finance Minister Korekiyo Takahashi, Grand Chamberlain Kantaro Suzuki, Inspector General of Military Education Jotaro Watanabe, and former cabinet minister Nobuaki Makino, and took control of the premises of the National Diet Building, Ministry of War of Japan, and the General Staff Office. Seeking an imperial system of government directly ruled by the Emperor, this rebellion by young officers of the Imperial Way Faction was squashed on February 29, the fourth day. Nevertheless, it led to the mass resignation of the Okada Cabinet and the inauguration of the Konoe Cabinet in June 1937 of the following year. Through this incident, in one fell swoop, the military's intervention in government became much stronger.

In the spring of 1936, Yoshio entered Hiroshima City Misasa Jinjo Higher Elementary School. It seems he studied well and was often appointed the class monitor. Upon entering the higher curriculum section, he joined the sumo club as he was a boy who enjoyed both study and physical exercise.

On July 7, 1937 the following year, the Lugou Bridge Incident occurred, sparking the start of the Second Sino-Japanese War. The war was triggered that day by a nighttime incident. The Japanese army, carrying out nocturnal exercises, allegedly encountered enemy fire from the Chinese army encampment. This incident led to Japan rushing into full-scale war with China. The Japanese government's initial policy was for the Lugou Bridge Incident to be settled locally. However as the lines of engagement expanded, it developed into a situation that Japan could not withdraw from.

In 1938, Yoshio turned 8. On his birthday on February 5, the whole family enjoyed pork cutlets and croquettes. Then in March of that year, Seiji graduated from Hiroshima Prefectural Hiroshima First Middle School and was admitted to Hiroshima Senior High School Faculty of Letters English category. Hiroshi, who was continuing to be prone to sicknesses, was a student at the Hiroshima Prefectural Hiroshima Second Middle School. Because of the age gap between Yoshio and his elder brothers, it seems they did not often play together.

Meanwhile the mood of war in Japan increasingly permeated society. In April of that year, the National Mobilization Law was promulgated, and the government began to exercise control over various aspects of civilian life. Specifically, military demand was given top priority in order to stage an all-out war with China. The government wielded control over civilian life, especially on the personal economic level, but also in the areas of free speech and media.

On the evening of October 23 of that year, Grandfather Tomotaro, who had been leading a separate life, died at the other house in Rakurakuen. He was 73. His cause of death is unknown. By the time Yoshio was walking and talking, his grandfather had already left the Yokogawa-cho family home. He had visited his grandfather at the other house together with Seiji and Hiroshi on errands, but Yoshio wasn't that close to his grandfather. Neither Grandma Masa, nor anyone else in the family grieved that terribly for the dead grandfather who had called geishas to come round to party even from his sick bed. His funeral was a matter-of-fact affair.

In 1939, Yoshio turned 9. He entered the third grade at Misasa Jinjo Higher Elementary School and continued to be fit and well every day. Meanwhile, in Japan as a whole, the common people were losing freedoms in their life. In April, the Rice Distribution Control Law was enforced and rice transactions were taken over by a government-controlled distribution system. Then in August, a distribution system was introduced for fertilizer, and people were ordered to increase production of self-supplied fertilizer. As a result, sales of fertilizer decreased and Kiyosuke's work, which was operating a fertilizer company, began to be considerably affected.

Not just Japan but several countries throughout the world were on a mad dash toward war. On September 1, 1939, while Japan and China were in full-scale war in the Far East, the German Army without warning invaded Poland and the Second World War erupted. The Japanese Government admired Germany's overwhelming victory and began plotting to form an alliance with Germany. Then from this time onward, the enmity deepened between the axis countries of Japan, Germany and Italy and the allied countries United States, Britain, the Netherlands, Australia, etc.

Also in 1939, events occurred on the other side of the ocean in the United States that would determine Yoshio's fate. In August that year, U.S. physicist Leo Szilard, fearing that the Germans were developing nuclear weapons, sought the advice of fellow physicist Albert Einstein. He then put forward a case to President Franklin Roosevelt that the United States should also proceed with the development of nuclear weapons. Although the manufacturing technique for nuclear weapons had not been established at that time, this is said to have been the beginnings of the Manhattan Project that would commence in 1942.

It was no doubt difficult for Yoshio, who had not yet turned 10, to fathom the wars that were occurring on the Chinese continent and in the far-off countries of Europe. Naturally, the education he was receiving at his school was fostering a spirit of nationalism with respect to the war against China, and one wonders how much thought Yoshio gave to the war that Japan was engaged in. As it was an age of the militarist boy when boys dreamed of becoming soldiers and facing the battlefield once they grew up, it would not have been surprising if Yoshio held such feelings.

However, setting him apart from the other many boys, there was an obstacle preventing him going to the battlefield as a soldier. Still only 9 years of age, he had become considerably nearsighted. Therefore, without glasses his lifestyle had become quite impaired. As his mother Futayo had also been nearsighted, which had been rare for girls, and Seiji had worn glasses since middle school as well, it was probably hereditary. On December 19 of that year, Yoshio received a pair of glasses from Tamaya Opticians, located on Kinza Street, Hiroshima. From then on, he led his life always wearing glasses.

In 1940, Yoshio was 10. On September 27 of that year, the Tripartite Pact between Japan, Germany and Italy was concluded. Japan was gradually getting more entwined in complex interests not just with China but also with various countries around the globe, and it was falling into a predicament with no way out. Although it had signed a non-aggression pact with the Soviet Union, its enmity and tensions with various countries such as the United States, Britain, the Netherlands, and Australia were escalating.

Entering 1940, it was becoming clearer that resource shortages were gradually becoming more serious in Japan. The government responded by taking control of the distribution of various items. Rice was among these items. The government took control of rice distribution from that year, and from the next year, it enforced a passbook system for the entire rice distribution of Hiroshima Prefecture. The sale of rice was put under the control of the Prefectural Food Authority, and the distribution per single adult per day was 432 ml.

Living under this austere civilian life, Yoshio's family was lucky. Because the family operated a fertilizer company, it was easy to obtain rice and other food items. The level of abundance in food enjoyed by Yoshio's family was in stark contrast to the experience of other families. On Yoshio's birthday on February 5 of that year, pork cutlets were served at the dinner table, and on Hiroshi's birthday on February 19, it was sushi. Then on Seiji's birthday, on July 19, it was cutlets and omelet. To serve such cuisine on the dinner table in those days was an extravagance that an ordinary family would not have been able to contemplate.

On October 27, the entire family went to the northern Hiroshima Prefecture to the ravine Sandan-kyo for a recreational trip to view the autumn leaves. This suggests Yoshio's family was doing a bit better than just coping with life overall. Seiji, enjoying the free atmosphere of Senior High School, was an avid movie goer, and he went to the cinema almost every day. He also joined the baseball team and applied himself to sports

In 1941, Yoshio turned 11. He was now in sixth grade at Misasa Jinjo Higher Elementary School. As his grades were good, it was decided that he would sit the entrance examination for the Hiroshima Prefectural Hiroshima First Middle School (called First Middle School for short), which was where Seiji went.

That spring, Seiji graduated from Hiroshima Prefectural Senior High School. He was admitted to the Law Faculty of Kyoto Imperial University and went to live in a boarding house in Kyoto. In the family home, Yoshio was now just living with one brother, his second eldest brother Hiroshi. Hiroshi had a weak constitution. In 1939 when Yoshio turned 9, Hiroshi transferred from the Hiroshima Prefectural Hiroshima Second Middle School in Kanonmachi (now Kanonmachi Nishi Ward, Hiroshima) to Soutoku Middle School in Kusunoki-cho. Hiroshi's poor health over this period meant that he was frequently absent from school.

Yoshio as a boy (Seiji at back, Hiroshi on right)
Provided by Toshinori Kanaya

As a result, he soon left Soutoku Middle School midway through and lived a life of convalescence at home.

Maybe it was because of Hiroshi's sickly constitution, but Yoshio found it easier to seek advice about the middle school entrance exam from his eldest brother Seiji, who was living in Kyoto, rather than from second eldest brother Hiroshi, who was living together with Yoshio. Yoshio mailed his grades report card to Seiji's place, and asked for detailed advice concerning studying techniques.

<Letter stamped May 30, 1941>
(Sender) Yoshio Kanaya, 33 Yokogawa-cho 1-chome, Hiroshima
(Addressee) Seiji Kanaya, C/O Yoshio Ozawa, 6 Yoshidakamioji-cho, Sakyo Ward, Kyoto

Dear Big Brother,
How are you? Today, I am sending my grades report.
I'm rather hopeless at reading. Arithmetic is my best subject.
From tomorrow (May 30), the mid-term exams run for five days.
I will put my head down and get good scores.
I will send my grades report again next month.
I have joined the sumo club and am practicing hard.
On the 15th, there is an inter-school tournament at Hirose Kokumin School.
On the 22nd, there is the all-school inter-school tournament at Sogo Ground.
I will write again next month. Stay well!
ITCHU!
From Yoshio

From that letter, we know that Yoshio was regularly sending his grades report cards as a way of seeking advice from his ten-years-older brother about how to study. Yoshio energetically applied himself to both study and sport, and he was a lively boy.

There is an anecdote about Yoshio after he had joined the sumo club. One day, when his first cousins came to visit from Otake, Yoshio, in a playful mood, appeared in front of everyone in sumo garb. It caused

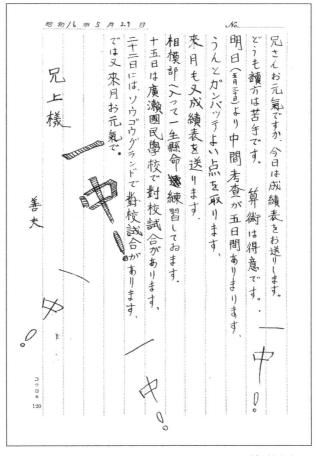

Yoshio's letter
Provided by Toshinori Kanaya

everyone to burst out laughing. One of the cousins, Yoshie, who was 14, wrote to Seiji in a letter, "Yoshi showed us a ridiculous sight, it was so funny."

Incidentally, at around that time, Yoshio was pouring an almost abnormal amount of enthusiasm into a certain activity. He had a strong interest in airplanes and making model airplanes. Exactly what brought about this interest is unclear, but it was most likely triggered by an encounter with a real airplane as shown in the photo on the previous page.

Yoshio photographed on a seaplane
Provided by Toshinori Kanaya

Even while preparing for the entrance exam to get into middle school in the following year, his enthusiasm for making model airplanes only increased. In June that year, he wrote to Seiji requesting that he buy a design drawing for a model airplane when he was coming home.

<Letter stamped June 16, 1941>
(Sender) Yoshio Kanaya, 33 Yokogawa-cho 1-chome, Hiroshima
(Addressee) Seiji Kanaya, C/O Yoshio Ozawa, 6 Yoshidakamioji-cho, Sakyo Ward, Kyoto

Dear big brother. It's good to hear you are well.

I'm also well. About that plane you wrote about with the front and back propellers that was in the model airplane shop in Kyoto, they have that one in Hiroshima as well. Yesterday was Sunday, and I went with the man from the airplane shop to the Eastern Parade Ground to fly a glider (wings 2 meters, fuselage 1 meter 20 centimeters). It lifted up three times. On the second time, the wing broke a little, and the fuselage broke a bit as well. But on the third time, it rose up and then it just fell to bits in the air. The wing broke, and fuselage hanger flew off, the longeron was all messed up and the silk was in pieces. It was a sorrowful sight. And so, when you come home next, if there is an interesting design drawing (preferably a glider), please buy it for me. A wing length of about 1 meter. But not the (Goppingen, Daimai G1, Maeda 6, Maeda 7, or Koshiki 6). For example, a tailless glider.

Keep well! (Or in English, "Guddo Bai") ITCHU!

For an 11-year-old, Yoshio had a surprising level of knowledge about airplanes. The technical words such as "hanger," "longeron," "silk," and "tailless" would not be readily understood by people unfamiliar with the structure of airplanes. The letter reveals that Yoshio had already obtained considerable knowledge about airplanes. Then, as time went on, his passion for aircraft appeared only to strengthen. After being admitted to middle school, it by no means weakened. It was because of this obsession that in his second year, he failed his grades. Ironically, it was this event that sealed Yoshio's fate.

In this way, Yoshio was a boy enthusiastic about not only study and sport, but also building model airplanes. But as he had been nearsighted ever since he was a young child and had begun wearing glasses when he was nine years old, he was not going to be able to become an airplane pilot, which was every boy's dream at that time. Yoshio was probably totally engrossed in creating model airplanes precisely because he would not be able to take the controls of an airplane and fly in the sky himself.

At the same time that Yoshio was either studying hard for the entrance exam for middle school or enthusiastically creating model airplanes, life in Japan was becoming more and more severe. While continuing the war with China, Japan had embraced a vision called the Greater East Asia Co-Prosperity Sphere. Japan's strategy was to advance southwards to liberate South East Asian countries from colonial powers. To obstruct the expansion of Japan's range of power, the United States, Britain, China and the Netherlands were strengthening the economic blockade. This was the so-called ABCD encirclement. Specifically, on July 28, 1941, the United States repelled the Japanese army's advance into French Indochina, and decided to place a full-scale prohibition of oil exports to Japan. Then, as the Britain and the Netherlands followed the United States' lead, Japan, which was nearly entirely reliant on foreign countries such as the United States for its oil supply, instantly found itself on the brink of a crisis. Moreover, the United States assisted China by applying China to the Lend-Lease Act and thereby was able to supply military equipment. Through these actions, Japan was driven into the unavoidable situation of waging war against not only China but also these countries.

On September 6 of that year, in an imperial conference with the Emperor, it was decided to "immediately pass a resolution for the outbreak of war against the United States in an event of no prospect of [Japan's] requests being carried out by early October by means of diplomatic negotiations." War with the United States had become imminent. Prime Minister Fumimaro Konoe, who was striving to avoid such war, held confidential talks with the American Ambassador to Japan, Joseph Grew and urged for a top-level meeting between Japan and the United States. But the American side refused. In relation to this, Prime Minister Konoe had been seeking the realization of Japan and United States negotiations with the condition of troop withdrawal from China. However, as the Army Minister Hideki Tojo was opposed to troop withdrawal from China, as there was pressure for either mass resignation or the outbreak of war with the United States based on the outline of Imperial policy, on October 16, the Konoe Cabinet, having exhausted all measures, resigned on mass. Then on October 18, the Tojo Cabinet was inaugurated and Japan had become a state in which the Japanese Army presided over the national administration.

On November 20, the Japanese Government proposed, as a final diplomatic proposal, conditions such as Japan not making military advance into various regions other than French Indochina, and the United States supplying aviation fuel to Japan, but President Roosevelt rejected the Japanese proposal. The United States' counter proposal was for Japan to make a full troop withdrawal from the Chinese mainland and French Indochina, that the United States would not recognize civilian governments that are puppet regimes of Japan, and that it would not recognize the Tripartite Pact. This counter proposal—known as the Hull Note—was considered by the Japanese Government as the United States' final proposal, and war against the United States became even more unavoidable.

On December 1, the Tojo Cabinet resolved to commence war with the United States at an imperial conference on December 8. Then, before daybreak, the Japanese Army landed on the Malay Peninsula and engaged with the British Indian Army. The Japanese Navy Air Force attacked U.S. naval vessels and the U.S. military base located at Pearl Harbor on Oahu Island of the U.S. Territory of Hawaii.

On December 8, when the Japan U.S. war started, Yoshio was 11. I wonder how he was feeling while listening to the radio breaking the news that Japan was at war with the United States. Seiji, in Kyoto, was at university, attending a class on International Law that had started at 3.00 p.m. Seiji, who learned of the war from the professor before the start of the lecture, was stunned by the news and unable to listen to the lecture for some time. Seiji had not once contemplated the notion that Japan would start a war with the United States and Britain. After the lecture, when he was returning to his boarding house, there was a bulletin posted on the back of the university gate stating that Japan was at war with the United States. That day, in his diary, Seiji wrote that he couldn't believe it to be true and was unable to settle down and listen to the lecture.

Chapter 2 Hiroshima First Middle School

In 1942, Yoshio turned 12. That year, Yoshio, who had sat the entrance exam for Hiroshima Prefectural Hiroshima First Middle School, went to the school on March 9 for the posting of results. Then, when he looked on the register of accepted students posted on the notice board, he found his number, 458, printed there. Yoshio had been accepted into the middle school of his wish. That year, the school accepted 250 students.

Hiroshima Prefectural Hiroshima First Middle School (Hiroshima First Middle School) was founded in 1877 as Hiroshima Prefectural Middle School from its predecessor, the National School of Foreign Languages, which was founded in 1874. It was the oldest middle school in the prefecture. The school motto was "austerity and fortitude," and it encouraged students to aim to be a both a good warrior and a good scholar. It was one of the top five middle schools in terms of its rate of academic advancement to top-class schools, with many of the students advancing to the Naval Academy, and the Military Academy. Furthermore, the school's sports clubs were also magnificent. For example, the soccer

Hiroshima Prefectural Hiroshima First Middle School
Provided by Toshinori Kanaya

club won the 18th National All-Schools Tournament in 1936 and won again in the 21st Tournament in 1939. The soccer club and other sports clubs would regularly make it through to the national all-schools tournament.

Belonging to a school steeped in such fine tradition, the students of Hiroshima First Middle School proudly held their heads high. Their pride was cultivated by this school's unique education policy. The teachers and students called this the "First Middle School spirit." This education policy also meant that it wasn't particularly easy for new students.

The new students, on the day of their admission ceremony were given instructions about the school rules. Specifically, "Students are expected to always patriotically carry out the Imperial will of the Emperor's word and Imperial edicts relating to education. If it is required of them, they are to repay the favor of the Emperor as a useful asset of the state, and they are to repay the favor of their parents." Moreover, in order to acquire the spirit of "austerity and fortitude," the daily life of students was regulated by strict rules. When outside their home, students had to wear school uniform. In fact, students were prohibited from wearing private attire while outside their home. Even if accompanied by a parent or elder sibling, etc., students were prohibited from cinemas and cafes. Wrist watches and fountain pens were absolutely forbidden, and students were not allowed to wear overcoats or gloves over their uniforms even in the winter. Students living in the city's central circle had to walk to and from school, while students living further afield, had to walk to school from either Hiroshima, Yokogawa, or Koi stations. Yoshio, who walked to First Middle School from his home in Yokogawa-cho, waited at Yokogawa Station for the out-of-city students coming to school on the Kabe Line to alight, and together in rank and file, they would cross Yokogawa Bridge, walk through the back of Teramachi, cross the Aioi Bridge and past the front of the Industrial Promotion Hall. They would then enter Sarugaku-cho and walk down either Otemachisuji or Onomichi-cho, or Shioyacho, then cut across the rail tracks, turn left at the Asano Library and arrive at the First Middle School front gate marching in step.

The relationships of seniority were strictly followed at the school. There were rules on behavior in front of senior students and teachers, such as "When students encounter the principal or teachers, they must stop walking, bow, and if they receive a bow in return, they shall step back." and "Students shall exchange bows, with the junior student bowing first." This meant that when students met teachers and senior students, such as when going to or from school, they were expected to stop and bow. If by chance a student was rude to a senior student, the student was either immediately punched, or called the next day to receive a severe scolding and beating. There was one anecdote of a certain first grader who responded to a First Middle School student coming his way by standing to attention and then bowing, only to later realize it was a fellow first grader. It was funny, but as everyone treated the issue so importantly, no one could laugh.

With these rules alone, the strictness of the school culture was daunting. But what made new students quake the most was the existence of a senior student called a "buin." The buin was decided by election from each grade, and many of the buin were chosen from students who were both excellent academically and on the A team of a sports club. The school assigned the buin the role of autonomously supervising the culture of the students as a whole, and they had tremendous power.

When the new students had finished the admission ceremony, they were quickly ushered into the kendo dojo under orders from the buin, and all students had to kneel with buttocks on heels. Then, holding bamboo swords, the buin would stomp the floor and walk around the tense straight-postured new students. To one student at a time, a buin would ask,

"For what purpose did you enter First Middle School?"

To which, the student would reply with statements such as,

"To study hard and become a valuable person."

The buin would suddenly deliver consecutive slaps and yell,

"Don't be an idiot! You have come to learn the First Middle School spirit and become a patriot. That is First Middle School!"

For the young boys aged about 12, these teenagers about 5 years older than them appeared like adults. So naturally, this initiation by the buin shortly after the admission ceremony not only scared the new students, but it also hammered the school culture into them.

The crucial part of this educational policy was to ensure that the students entering First Middle School would have the First Middle School spirit planted in them under the unique guidance of their teachers

Yoshio upon entering Hiroshima First Middle School
Provided by Toshinori Kanaya

and senior students. Of course the school was also ferociously passionate about studying, and there seemed to be a test for some subject every day. The results of these tests would be posted on the wall with the students listed according to test results. Each year, somewhere between 10 and 20 percent of students failed their year. The new students had little time to savor the joy of having been accepted into First Middle School as they had to desperately work their hardest every day to cope with school life.

I don't know how well Yoshio was able to adapt to this school culture after entering First Middle School. At any rate, he had started school life at the middle school he had wanted to go to.

In the middle of the night on April 30, soon after Yoshio entered the school, Grandma Masa suddenly passed away. Apparently it was heart failure. She was 70. Out of her grandchildren, Masa had only ever doted over Seiji. Therefore, Yoshio's feelings about her passing would have brought similar dispassionate feelings to how he felt when his grandfather died. After receiving the telegram to tell him of Masa's death, Seiji, who was in Kyoto, arrived home on May 2, and the funeral for Masa was held on the May 4. The funeral was an orderly affair uninterrupted by any tremendous weeping or wailing from among the family. On the May 11, Seiji went back to Kyoto and once more it became quiet inside the house. For Yoshio, life at home comprised four people: himself, his parents, and his second eldest brother Hiroshi.

Meanwhile, at the beginning of 1942, the time when Yoshio entered First Middle School, Japanese society was excited over early military successes in the war against the United States, which had started from the previous year. Japan, which had entered a state of war with the Allies, notably with the United States in December of 1941, continued to hold advantage in various regions at the time, and it had expanded this sphere of influence from South East Asia to include all areas of the Pacific Ocean. However, this advantage was a passing moment, and by halfway through 1942, contrary to the expectations among the Japanese public, the tide of war gradually began turning.

On April 18, 16 B-25 bombers took off from U.S.S Hornet, an aircraft carrier of the United States Navy located in waters close to Japan in the Pacific Ocean. The bombers raided Tokyo and surrounding cities. It was the first aerial attack on Japan by the U.S. military. As the Japanese public morale had been whipped up by their country's run of successes in the series of battles with the United States, it came as huge shock when Japan's capital was on the receiving end of an aerial attack by American bombers.

Then beginning in May in the South Pacific Ocean, the Japanese military began an offensive to attack Port Moresby in south-east New Guinea, and the aircraft carrier task force of the Japanese Navy and the aircraft carrier task force of the U.S. Navy engaged in battle in the Coral Sea. Known as Battle of the Coral Seal, this battle resulted in both sides receiving losses, including the loss of aircraft carriers. As a result of the battle, the Japanese military was unable to attack Port Moresby, which thwarted its advance in this region.

Then in June, in the Battle of Midway, the Japanese Navy suffered heavy losses, which included the loss of four aircraft carriers. As a result of this battle, just half a year since the outbreak of war between Japan and the United States, the tables had turned for the United States and Japanese militaries with a reversal of the positions of attacker and defender. These setbacks by the Japanese military, however, were unknown by the Japanese public. The news from the radio and newspapers continued to report to the public as if the Japanese military was enjoying consecutive victories on the battlefield.

For Yoshio, now a middle school student, there was one more change in the family. Not long after the passing of Grandma Masa, his second eldest brother Hiroshi, aged 20, went over to Manchukuo. Having always possessed a weak constitution, Hiroshi had been convalescing at home since dropping out of school midway through Soutoku Middle School. However it seems that this was something that he set his mind to do. He decided to join the Manchukuo Railway Youth Corps, which was actively recruiting at the time. Worried about his weak constitution, his parents were opposed to him going, but it did not change Hiroshi's mind. He had his own thoughts concerning the matter. Despite the sentiment of the Japanese public riding high from victories in the war against the United States, most Japanese struggled with the hard daily life of wartime Japan. It seems that Hiroshi felt guilty that he could only live inside his house, unable to do anything because of his weak constitution.

In the summer of that year when Hiroshi traveled to Manchukuo, a massive typhoon known as Typhoon Suonada caused a serious disaster in the Hiroshima area. In the middle of the night of August 27, Typhoon No. 16 passed through the Yamaguchi area, and the regions that faced the Suonada Sea and Hiroshima Bay were inundated by flooding due to the high tide and strong southerly winds, which destroyed a dike on reclaimed land called Shinkai located on the Hiroshima Bay coastline. It was a terrible calamity with thousands of homes inundated or destroyed and 1,158 dead or missing. It also caused the Sanyo Railway to stop running for 10 days.

Despite this great damage wrought by the Suonada Typhoon to the Hiroshima area, the Yokogawa-cho area, where Yoshio's home was located, fortunately managed to avoid the serious damage. Even though Ota River, which ran in front of the home, considerably swelled, the house escaped from being flooded.

Meanwhile, the course of the war over this time was gradually taking a turn for the worse. In August, U.S. forces landed on the island of Guadalcanal in the Solomon Islands and took control of the Japanese military airstrip. In reaction to this, the Japanese military, aiming to reclaim Guadalcanal, attempted a counter-attack by sending in army forces under the guidance of fleet support, but failed. Through the course of many battles in the seas around the Solomon Islands, the battle for this sea territory turned into a quagmire, and the fighting power of the Japanese military was gradually exhausted.

Also around this time, a new weapon was being developed in the United States under orders from President Roosevelt. The organization developing this weapon was established under the front of a department named Manhattan Engineering District. However, its real function was to secretly develop the atomic bomb. The development of nuclear weapons that Leo Szilard had suggested to President Roosevelt was finally being made a reality. The person put in charge of this project was Brigadier General Lesley Groves, and the chief scientist in charge of development was physicist Robert Oppenheimer. The research laboratory that would carry out development was chosen to be located at Los Alamos in the State of New Mexico. The dreaded weapon that would rob Yoshio of his life three years later had begun its first embryonic movement.

For Yoshio, although there had been changes in the family, such as the death of his grandmother and his second eldest brother going to Manchukuo, it was the year in which he was admitted into his dream school, First Middle School. As such, these were hope-filled days for him. However, perhaps due to his long-held care-free personality, since starting middle school, he was unable to apply himself to his school study. Meanwhile, building model aircraft, which had been a passion when he was still at elementary school, became an even greater passion. Also at that time, military authorities had collected middle school students together and held flight training of gliders at the Eastern Parade Ground. Their purpose was probably to cultivate future airmen. Although he didn't dream of flying an aircraft because of his near-sightedness, he was still enthusiastic for gliders, and whenever he found time, day in, day out, he would be doing glider practice with classmates.

Perhaps for this reason, Yoshio's grades for his first trimester were not very good. When his father Kiyosuke, who was passionate about the education of his children, found out about the grades, he scolded Yoshio for his poor study. Nevertheless, Yoshio did not seem to be that concerned.

Worried about Yoshio's blasé attitude toward life, Kiyosuke wrote a letter to Seiji in Kyoto to urge Seiji to talk to Yoshio about why his grades were poor. In response to Kiyosuke's letter, Seiji replied as follows.

<Letter stamped November 26, 1942>
(Sender) Seiji Kanaya, C/O Sango Matsumoto, 54/128 Shimogamo Miyazaki-cho, Sakyo Ward, Kyoto
(Addressee) Kiyosuke Kanaya, 33 Yokogawa-cho 1-chome, Hiroshima

Dear Father. Concerning the matter of Yoshio's poor grades. If all his subjects were poor, it is a matter of concern. However, if, for example, literature and history, etc. were poor but mathematics and science, etc. were good, I don't think there is much cause for worry. I think that only getting 6 points in some subjects but getting 10 points in other subjects is a better outcome than obtaining 8 points in each subject. Considering Yoshio's future, Rather than being an average person who has no special aptitude in anything, I think that holding exceptional talent in one thing would be better for society, the country, and the world. I believe genius refers to a person who is particularly outstanding in one talent. So while I think we should make sure that he does not fail those subjects he does not excel in, as that would be a problem, we should also work out how to get him to vastly improve in the other subjects he is good at. His enthusiasm for model airplanes is not necessarily something to be reproached. If this is simply nothing but "play," then there is no point to it. If however, this develops into interests in gliders and actual aircraft, and it gets him interested in the assembly of aircraft, in engine-based flight and in weather,

46

etc., then it could lead him to further study in mathematics, physics, chemistry and meteorology, and it may become a path to a future aircraft crewman or engineer. Needless to say, the school also gets the students to make model airplanes and fly gliders. My point is that the underside of every strong point has a weak point and the underside of every weak point has a strong point. There is no point in choosing a cure that's worse than the disease. I think we should continue to allow those strong points that fit with his innate personality to grow more and more. If Yoshio is to follow a career of science in the future, then mathematics, languages, science, etc. are very important. But I don't think that literature and history etc. are really that necessary for him. They are things he should know as ordinary general knowledge, and even if he delves deeper into these, it should be done out of his own interest.

I will not go as far as saying I think interest is the most important thing for study, but if we overly forced Yoshio to do the subjects he is not good at, it would result in him hating study. Conversely, if he has some kind of subject that he is good at, he will develop an interest in it. Then study will become interesting, and this will cause him to naturally study better at the subjects he is not good at. This is something that you have also said, father.

Another thing that I think you, Father, have experienced is that when people reach a certain age, they awake to what is called the ego. At this age, a person, who has lived their life thus far as their parents' belonging without really questioning, starts to become conscious of a thing called self. Armed with this self, the person starts conveying a will to go a separate way from the parents. Although this may appear risky from the parents' perspective, the child is developing the wish to be no longer small and weak but instead to become self-supporting and independent. If this is interfered with and suppressed from above, a rebellious spirit can arise. Putting aside whether this is good or bad, if this is the person's nature, then it is impossible to avoid. Let him naturally be, and if the situation gets really bad, then it will be necessary to apply the brakes. (Rest of letter omitted.)

Seiji had appealed for his father to understand this way of thinking concerning Yoshio's attitude toward study. After reading this reply from Seiji, Kiyosuke remained unhappy with the situation. He replied saying that as Yoshio's grades were poor in all his subjects, and he was unable to share the same understanding that Seiji conveyed.

I don't know whether he was aware of these exchanges between his father and eldest brother, but Yoshio's lifestyle continued as before. Meanwhile, November came around, and Hiroshi, who had joined the Manchukuo Youth Corps in Manchukuo, had returned to Japan. Not unexpectedly, illness-prone Hiroshi had deemed life in Manchukuo impossible. The family home once again comprised four members: Yoshio, his parents, and his second eldest brother. Hiroshi's physical condition was poorly since he returned. He had a slight fever nearly every day, and was often confined to the house.

The new year came, and although the time for advancement to second grade was drawing near, Yoshio still was not taking to study, remaining totally engrossed in making model airplanes and practicing gliders. This was despite the fact that as a student of the prestigious First Middle School—famous in the Prefecture as a stepping-stone to the best schools and for its Spartan education—neglect of school work was putting Yoshio at risk of failing and being denied advancement to second year. All too aware of this fact, Kiyosuke hired a home tutor. The tutor was a student at the Hiroshima Bunrika University by the name of Suzuki. It seems that Yoshio took a liking to this young man's gentle character and meticulous teaching style, and from then on, he gradually applied himself to his studies.

<Letter stamped February 1943>
(Sender) Yoshio Kanaya, 33 Yokogawa-cho 1-chome, Hiroshima
(Addressee) Seiji Kanaya, C/O Sango Matsumoto, 128 Shimogamo
Miyazaki-cho, Sakyo Ward, Kyoto

Dear Big Brother,
How are you? Everyone, including me, are well. My tutor Mr.
Suzuki is kind, and a really good teacher. He is also a top swimmer.
My study is as it always is, and nothing much has changed at
school. I heard that Mr. Doi is resigning at the end of the third
term. Mr. Kanroku sends his regards.
Did you get my note the other day? Any time is fine, so send it
quickly. Please.

The "Mr. Doi" mentioned in the letter was Toshio Doi, the English
Teacher, and "Mr. Kanroku" was the drillmaster Kanroku Toyoshima, he
was Seiji's teacher when Seiji was at First Middle School.

Japan's position in the war against the United States, which started
in December 1941, continued to only worsen throughout the second half
of 1942. In February 1943, about ten thousand officers and men of the
Japanese military withdrew from Guadalcanal, and the hard-fought
battle for Guadalcanal was declared over with the Japanese military
defeated.

Then on April 18, Admiral Isoroku Yamamoto, commander-in-
chief of the combined fleet, died in battle when the naval aircraft he was
in traveling in was shot down while flying over Bougainville on route to
monitor the frontline base in the south. However, as the Imperial
Headquarters did not publicize Commander-in-chief Yamamoto's death,
it was not until May 21 that the public heard the news. As he was a
Japanese Naval hero, the news of his death was a morale blow to the
public, who had believed Japan had been continually winning battles.

Upon learning of Commander-in-chief Yamamoto's death in battle, Seiji wrote the following in his diary on May 22. "In an instant, all is silent."

Also in May, at Attu Island on the far western edge of the Aleutian Islands, a fierce battle unfolded between a Japanese military guard and U.S. forces who had landed. On May 29, the Japanese military guard of 2,600 men was nearly entirely wiped out. The Japanese military suffered an accumulation of defeats like this one on various fronts. The fighting power and materiel of the Japanese Army was depleting at a whole new level. Inside Japan, however, there were no air raids by U.S. aircraft and on the surface, the people were carrying out daily life calmly.

Meanwhile, up until February of that year, Yoshio had apparently got on well with his home tutor Mr. Suzuki and even applied himself to his studies. Perhaps as a result of this, he safely advanced to second grade. However, in June, for some reason, he refused to go to school.

One day, Yoshio announced to his parents,

"I'm not going to go to school anymore."

Kiyosuke asked him why not, but Yoshio didn't give an answer.

At the time, Seiji, who happened to be home at the time, wrote about Yoshio in his diary.

June 6 (Sunday). *Vater* (Father), *Mutter* (Mother), Hiroshi and I discussed that night about what to do about Yoshio.

June 7 (Monday). In the evening, Hiroshi and I asked Yoshio of his thoughts. He answered that he did not wish to return to school. (But I could not determine whether or not that was his true feeling.)

June 9 (Wednesday). Rain. I supervised Yoshio's preparation for Chinese literature. I went to bed at 10 p.m.

In the end, this matter was a temporary event and Yoshio resumed going to school shortly afterward. While only speculation, given Yoshio's innocent care-free nature, the reason for his refusal to go to school was unlikely to be due to a poor showing of academic performance. Perhaps he was finding difficult to cope with First Middle School's strict Spartan educational culture.

The summer came, and once again it was typhoon season. While serious damage occurred in the Hiroshima area in August of the previous year due to Typhoon Suonada, in July of that year, large-scale flooding was caused by the effect of typhoons and the like.

First, in July, an active *baiu* front caused damage. Inside Hiroshima prefecture, there were 92 dead or missing persons, 332 fully or partially destroyed homes, 1,846 homes flooded above floor level, and 126 bridges washed out. Then, in September, the effect of Typhoon No. 26 caused rain to settle in on the 18th. This rain continued and gradually intensified until the typhoon hit land at Okayama Prefecture on the 20th. The massive rainfall caused swelling of the rivers. The rivers overflowed downstream of Kabe, inundating the entire plains, including the Hiroshima city area. Some parts of the city suffered floodwater more than 1 meter high. As a result, about 50 houses inside the city were washed away, 11,545 houses were flooded, and 36 bridges were washed out.

The flooding in September wreaked damage on Yoshio's home as well this time. Ota River in front of the home began surging from the afternoon of September 20th, the water level rose above the river walls and soon flooded the home as the level rose above the home's floor level. There was much bustle, with the whole family, including Seiji who had just returned home from Kyoto, carrying furniture and the like upstairs at the house, while at the company nearby, employees carted office documents and equipment to the warehouse. Sandbags were laid around the home, but these were unable to stop the encroaching floodwater. There was also a power blackout, so candles provided lighting throughout the night.

On the following day, the 21st, the family scooped up the mud that had been carried into the house by the flood water and removed the remaining water from the basement. Because the floodwaters remained on the road in front of the house, a raft had to be used for transport. On the 22nd, the water began to subside and the family was able to rest.

That day, Seiji's friend from Senior High School, Yoshitake paid a visit and said that Prime Minister Tojo had announced in a radio broadcast a stop of the temporary exemption from conscription of students. This meant that students aged 20 years or over at university or higher-education specialist schools other than science, engineering, medicine and teacher training had to enlist on December 1 after undergoing a medical examination for extraordinary conscription. As Seiji was 23 at the time, he too would now join the military.

Seiji underwent the conscription medical examination on October 29 and passed with No.1 standard of fitness. On November 17, he graduated from Kyoto University, which had been brought forward, and then after attending a send-off party in Hiroshima on November 30, he headed for Shimonoseki by train on that day. After arriving at Shimonoseki, Seiji crossed over to Mutsure Island 5 kilometers offshore from Takezaki Port, and joined the Western Army 8063rd Division as an air defense soldier to be stationed at the anti-aircraft gun site in the island hills.

Seiji's enlistment as a soldier was considered by Yoshio to be a natural turn of events. Conscription was an inevitable path for young men in Japan at that time. Yoshio, like all the other boys, was a militarist boy. He did not doubt that Japan would be victorious as he had been thoroughly educated as a youth about the divine nation of Japan that did not lose. As a boy in that time and place, Yoshio considered it natural that he and his brothers would put forward their life for country and face the battlefield.

<Letter stamped December 9, 1943>
(Sender) Yoshio Kanaya, 33 Yokogawa-cho 1-chome, Hiroshima

(Addressee) Seiji Kanaya, Wada Unit, Western Army 8063rd Division C/O Shimonoseki Post Office

Dear Eldest Brother. It is with much joy that we hear that you are well. I too am well, and I am applying myself to my school work every day, so you need not worry about that. By the way, could you tell me which is the Brownie film that doesn't have a very wide width of poor sensitivity? Thanks.

Go forth then soldier
No regrets even in death,
Young cherry blossom
Sincerely Yours,
Yoshio
December 8, 1943

The Student Mobilization Order had not been issued for middle schools. Nevertheless, beginning from that year, even the middle schools were allocating less time to class work and increasing the time spent on manual labor outside the school to more than that spent on school work.

<Letter stamped December 14, 1943>
(Sender) Yoshio Kanaya, 33 Yokogawa-cho 1-chome, Hiroshima
(Addressee) Seiji Kanaya, Wada Unit, Western Army 8063rd Division C/O Shimonoseki Post Office

Dear Eldest Brother Seiji,
Has there been any change? Father, Mother, Hiroshi and I are all well.
The second trimester is nearly over with classes finishing in several days' time. After that, we will head out to the farming villages to work for lodgings. I'm very eager to work for the nation.

With school as well, it's like I have finally taken notice this time, and I am really working hard. Although I am in second grade, it's a four-grade system, so because we are doing the equivalent of third grade in a five-grade system, everyone is spending our free time discussing the directions each of us should be taking. At any rate, because a third of our time is now labor, it seems we will hardly have any lesson time in January, February and March next year.

By the way, all my friends are talking about heading in the direction of the Air Force or being related to the navy, etc., but both the Air Force and the Navy are no good for me because of the strength of my nearsightedness. However for aircrew today, the navy is accepting people with eyesight of 0.8 left/right and 1.2 with both eyes. In the army, up to 0.6 is mostly acceptable. Currently, I am paying attention to adequate correction and using an optics company's correcting tool, but if you know of any other good methods, please let me know. Also as I have nearsightedness, which school do you think would be better? I am thinking the Army, or Naval Paymaster's School. I like the military, especially the navy. If you think any particular school is mostly good, please tell me. If I flunk out, I'll end up as an industrial soldier. I'm not too bad with a hammer. But then there wouldn't have been any purpose spending time and money going to middle school for four years. As I am going to school, I want to be able to use my head even a little better than now and sufficiently serve the country. I know you're busy Seiji, but please think about it for me.

What I have written probably sounds strange, but my conversations go nowhere with Father, and Hiroshi and I don't see eye to eye. So in the end, I am asking you. Please think about it. How is life in the military? As I have to consider military life, tell me what it's like. I'm sure it's a little different from your care-free university life. Ha ha...

By the way, in your (new) document draw, there was one roll of Sakura film. Shall we send it to get developed? You know it will get ruined if it is left there. And it's okay if you don't worry about future matters. Next Sunday, I plan to sort your books that arrived after. You can trust me. I won't do anything bad to them.

Also, could I have some 35 mm film? Can you please tell me the place where it is?

And as its getting cold, make sure you look after yourself as you serve our country.

Sincerely Yours,

Yoshio

December 23, 1943, 8 p.m.

On December 26, Yoshio and his father went to see Seiji who had joined the division on Mutsure Island. His mother Futayo did not come along because she was prone to motion sickness, and it was impossible for her to travel all the way to Shimonoseki. The two arrived at Mutsure Island, and after waiting at Hamaya Inn near the port, Seiji came to meet them. Not used to a soldier's lifestyle, Seiji apparently was struggling, but nevertheless he appeared to be in good spirits. Moreover, together with other ex-student soldiers, he was studying for the exam to become an officer cadet.

<Letter stamped December 27, 1943>

(Sender) Yoshio Kanaya, 33 Yokogawa-cho 1-chome, Hiroshima

(Addressee) Seiji Kanaya, Wada Unit, Western Army 8063rd Division C/O Shimonoseki Post Office

Dear Eldest Brother. It was a big relief to have met you yesterday and to see that you are in good spirits. We too arrived safely back at Yokogawa Station at 11 p.m. After we gave Mother a run-down of everything, she was very pleased.

This is something I wrote in the steam train.

"My Brother, without speaking of the cold, he guards our country."

"My Brother, without worrying of himself, he serves our Emperor."

On January 1, 1944, as Seiji had enlisted in December of the previous year, four family members welcomed in the new year together, Yoshio, his parents, and his second oldest brother Hiroshi. Then on February 5, Yoshio turned 14, and he was planning on advancing to third grade that spring.

<Letter stamped December 31, 1943>

(Sender) Yoshio Kanaya, 33 Yokogawa-cho 1-chome, Hiroshima

(Addressee) Seiji Kanaya, Wada Unit, Western Army 8063rd Division C/O Shimonoseki Post Office

Happy New Year!

I hope you welcomed in the new year in high spirits. Everyone here welcomed in the new year in a good mood, I was the most jovial of the family. With renewed energy, I will put in my best as a student in wartime both in my school work and in sport.

I am wishing today that you be protected in the hot, cold and any conditions.

Sincerely Yours,

Even though the state of the war was deteriorating daily, there were no air raids in the country at that stage, and daily life continued to appear calm on the surface.

Nevertheless, in September of the previous year, the government, considering the likelihood of a bomb raid by U.S. bombers on the military capital Hiroshima, began ordering compulsory evacuations of buildings from November. As part of these plans, the first-round of forced evacuation and demolition of buildings came into effect from May 2 for Kure and November 18 for Hiroshima.

The forced evacuation and demolition of buildings entailed the destruction and removal of buildings in entire zones to clear the land based on the Air Defense Act aimed at preventing the spread of fire from air raids by turning specified zones in the city into vacant land. The residents living inside the designated zones had to evacuate within one week after receiving notification. The pillars of the evacuated houses were cut with saws and the houses were pulled down with rope. Soldiers and adults of the Volunteer Fighting Corps did the work, and the mobilized middle school students participated. At the same time as the forced evacuation and demolition of buildings, the evacuation of student groups began.

Kiyosuke's company was in an even harsher business environment. On January 17, Kiyosuke attended the National Fertilizer Trade Association Conference as Hiroshima Prefecture's representative. There, he was stunned to learn that an integrated merger with the Ministry of Agriculture would take place, and that from August, the supply of fertilizer would be through a unified distribution. This meant that the trade of fertilizer was to be under the government's control.

Since around December in the previous year, Yoshio, who was in second grade school, had, in addition to school life, been lodging in rural districts and helping with work there. At the same time, he was doing his best with study as well.

<Letter stamped January 28, 1944>
(Sender) Yoshio Kanaya, 33 Yokogawa-cho 1-chome, Hiroshima
(Addressee) Seiji Kanaya, Wada Unit, Western Army 8063rd Division C/O Shimonoseki Post Office

Dear Eldest Brother. How are you? Things are the same for me. How was the exam? We are all anxious to know. Recently, I have been busy working. I went to a rural area for a week and just got back yesterday. The day after tomorrow, I will go to Kabe to work for one week there. I intend to work hard.

I am trying to study using your study method. It has made it much easier. Apparently the text books are going to change considerably. English and the like will probably be reduced. But in any case, I aim to work as hard as I can to get into a top-class school. Well then, take care of yourself.

Yours Sincerely, Yoshio

Seiji, who had been training hard as a new solider on Mutsure Island, took the officer cadet exam on January 25, and was accepted as a paymaster cadet on February 3. As he would be receiving apprentice officer training, he was reposted from Mutsure Island to the Western Army 46th Division in Fukuoka.

In mid-March, the Japanese military began engaging in battle with the Allied Army in the Burma area. Aiming to attack Imphal in the northeast of India, where the British Indian Army were stationed, the Japanese Army sent in about 90,000 soldiers and staged large-scale military operations. However, the campaign was recklessly planned with little thought given to how to supply provisions to the units. As a result, when the Allied Army staged a counter attack, it annihilated the Japanese military, which had run out of supplies. More than 30 thousand men and officers died, many from starvation. Finally, in July, the orders came to halt the campaign. It was a historic loss for the Japanese Army.

At that time, Yoshio had been applying himself to his studies with a mind to come back from a performance slump at school. However, he was unable to resist his interest in airplanes and, as always, he continued to be passionate about making model airplanes. As a result, his grades fell again, and at the school's grade advancement meeting in March, Yoshio was failed.

Even Hiroshi, normally one to stay quiet and not criticize others, was left thinking the outcome was not entirely unexpected and wrote to Seiji seeking his advice.

<Letter stamped March 29, 1944>
(Sender) Hiroshi Kanaya, 33 Yokogawa-cho 1-chome, Hiroshima
(Addressee) Seiji Kanaya, Hayashi Command 5 Western Army 46th Division, Fukuoka

Dear Elder Brother Seiji,
I read your letter. It was a relief for everyone knowing that you are well as always. We are all well, so please don't worry yourself about that.
Yoshio, as always, remains devoted to his model airplane making. Probably because of this, he has to repeat second grade. Yoshio, however, seems fine about it. I request that you give him some stern and encouraging words. Please do take care of yourself. Well, until next time.
Yours Sincerely,
Hiroshi

In spite of the worry he caused to Hiroshi and the other family members and regardless of the news of his failure, Yoshio, writing like it were someone else's affair, sent the following letter to Seiji.

<Letter stamped March 31, 1944>
(Sender) Yoshio Kanaya, 33 Yokogawa-cho 1-chome, Hiroshima
(Addressee) Seiji Kanaya, Hayashi Command 5 Western Army

46th Division, Fukuoka

Dear Eldest Brother Seiji,

How are you? As always, I am well. I'm writing because I was failed at the grade advancement meeting of March 16. At first I was a little surprised. I had intended to perform sufficiently but my aptitude was insufficient and it wasn't good that I was lackadaisical due to the first and second trimester grades being good. This time, rather than taking an average of first, second and third trimesters, apparently they only counted performance in the third trimester.

Oh well, even repeating a year, my February birthday ensures there won't be much of an age difference. My academic ability will probably improve. Rest assured that I will work hard next time.

They say third time lucky, but third time would be a worry wouldn't it. So I think it will be second time lucky. At the moment Aunty Maenaga and Hiroso are visiting. It's pretty rowdy.

By the way, among your films, there is a film roll "PAN F." What shall we do?

I think it will be ruined if we leave it another 3 months. Please reply. Stay well.

Yours Sincerely,

Yoshio

Even after he had been accepted as an officer cadet, Seiji, who was reposted from Mutsure Island to Fukuoka, had been carrying out grueling training, day in day out, to become an officer cadet. Coincidentally, he had been granted a leave pass from April 1 to 3, his first since joining the army, and for the first time in four months, he was able to spend time at home. Seiji boarded a carriage full of passengers squashed in like sardines at Shimonoseki station at 8:00 p.m. and arrived at Hiroshima station at 3:30 a.m. the following morning. He arrived home at 4:30 a.m. After he rang the doorbell at the front door, he was greeted by Yoshio. Who knows what kind of exchange the returning Seiji had with Yoshio, who had failed his school year. However, as it was Seiji, it was probably not an exceptional scolding.

Also at that time, as Hiroshi, now 22, was comparatively in good condition, he was going to convalesce at Etajima on Hiroshima Bay where he would stay and be a workhand at a piggery. It seems that Hiroshi felt compelled to relocate due to the societal tensions of the time. It was probably unbearable for Hiroshi that only he was idling away at home while most young people were going off to war and even those remaining were toiling with forced evacuation and demolition of buildings or labor mobilization. And everyone agreed that the warm island climate would be good for Hiroshi's body.

Meanwhile, Seiji who had finished his leave pass and returned to the division was struck with a high fever from May 1. Based on his subsequent medical examination, he was treated in-service for bronchitis but as his fever did not subside, he was hospitalized on May 6 at Shimonoseki Military Hospital.

Then on June 15 in the middle of the night while still hospitalized, Seiji asleep in his ward was woken by air raid sirens. When he looked outside the ward window, he started to hear the roaring of the enemy planes, and could see the searchlight beams intersecting each other like graph lines and the tracer ammunition soaring up into the sky like fireflies. Then he heard the sound of anti-aircraft shell exploding. The bombers were attacking across the water on the Kyushu coast either at Kokura or Yahata. After gazing at the air raid in motion, a B-29 bomber flew over the hospital. Seiji thought for a moment that the hospital would be bombed, but fortunately the plane just passed over without dropping a bomb.

The air raids on that day were carried out by 47 B-29 U.S. bombers with the mission to drop bombs on the Yahata Steel Works. These B-29s were part of 75 B-29s that had flown from a base in Chengdu, China. It was the first air raid on the Japanese main islands by the B-29. However, as the air raid on that day was an attack from a base located a long distance from Japan, it was unable to achieve sufficient military results.

The tides of war began to shift enormously. On the exact same day, the U.S. military began a landing on Saipan Island of the Mariana Islands in the northwest Pacific Ocean. The Japanese military tried to defend against the landing by the United States with a fleet that included nine aircraft carriers, but the United States staged a counter attack and the mechanized units of the Japanese Navy were annihilated. On July 7, the Japanese military guard on Saipan Island refused to surrender and fought to the last. Then, on July 23, the U.S. Army landed on Tinian Island. The U.S. Army, having occupied the islands, quickly created the world's largest airbase for bombers. This gave the U.S. military sufficient capability to conduct aerial bombing of the Japanese main islands using B-29 bombers. Moreover, this Tinian Island Airbase was the point of departure for the B-29 that carried the atomic bomb destined for Hiroshima.

After aerial attacks by U.S. bombers had begun on the Japanese main islands, Kiyosuke knew deep-down that Japan was losing the war. As Kiyosuke ran a fertilizer company and often travelled to various places in Japan to buy the raw materials for fertilizer, he witnessed for himself the damage from the air raids. Even in Hiroshima, bucket relays were conducted in each district as part of fire-fighting drills in preparation for aerial attacks. Moreover, defense drills using bamboo spears were being carried out seriously in anticipation of a U.S. invasion. Seeing all this, Kiyosuke knew there was no way that Japan was winning against the United States or other countries. Of course, the current tensions in society prevented Kiyosuke from openly speaking these views. Nor could he contemplate telling his sons that Japan was losing the war. Especially since Seiji had joined the service, and while the second oldest Hiroshi was leading a convalescent lifestyle due to his weak constitution, his fourth-born son Yoshio was at school believing Japan was winning the war and working hard as a mobilized laborer.

Having failed his year, Yoshio restarted life as a second grader. At that time, Hiroshima Prefecture had ordered the middle schools in the prefecture to mobilize student labor based on the "Guidelines for Establishment of Mobilization System for Students During Wartime" resolved by the cabinet in June of the previous year. Beginning from June at First Middle School, the fifth graders were mobilized to Kure Naval Arsenal in Kure, the fourth graders to Toyo Kogyo (now Mazda) in Fuchu in Aki District, and the third graders to Asahi Heiki in Minamikanon in the city of Hiroshima. However, as Yoshio was repeating second grade, he had still not received a mobilization order.

<Letter stamped July 2, 1944>
(Sender) Yoshio Kanaya, Yokogawa-cho 1-chome, Hiroshima
(Addressee) Seiji Kanaya, West Ward, No. 2 Hospital Building, Shimonoseki Military Hospital, C/O Shimonoseki Post Office

Dear Eldest Brother Seiji,

I am sorry I haven't written for so long. How have you been since last time? I have been doing lots of manual labor and my body has grown quite strong. The higher grades have all left to work at factories, and mostly they are working at military manufacturing. I really want to go working in such places as well. But, oh well, I will do my best going to the rural districts and helping with food production. I am wishing that you will have long-lasting energy and get strong.

Yours sincerely,

Yoshio

Soon after receiving this letter from Yoshio, Seiji was discharged from Shimonoseki Military Hospital. He was reassigned from the unit in Fukuoka back to the Western Army 8063rd Division on Mutsure Island.

<Letter stamped September 16, 1944>
(Sender) Yoshio Kanaya, Yokogawa-cho 1-chome, Hiroshima
(Addressee) Seiji Kanaya, Ikebe Unit, Western Army 8063rd Division C/O Shimonoseki Post Office

Dear Eldest Brother Seiji,

I am sorry for not writing for so long. It was a relief that you have since recovered. Things are the same as always with me. Please don't worry about me. Hiroso has visited while on leave. We also will soon be going to a factory at end of the month or in mid-October. I have decided to really work hard. I aim to go to the Army Paymaster's School. I am going to make sure I become a person that the future Far East can rely on. It will be getting cold soon, so be sure to look after yourself.

Yours Sincerely,

Yoshio

At First Middle School, the students in third grade and above had been away since June for labor mobilization in accordance with the Student Mobilization Order. Then in October, the second grade students were ordered to mobilize as well. Among the mobilization destinations for the second graders, class 17 went to Hiroshima Airline Company in Takasu, Furuta-cho Hiroshima (Takasu, Nishi Ward, Hiroshima), and then in February in the following year, class 18 went to Kansai Kousakujo in Funairi-Kawaguchi-cho, Hiroshima (Funairi-Kawaguchi-cho, Naka Ward, Hiroshima) and the remaining three classes 16, 19, 20 were mobilized to Toyo Kogyo.

<Letter stamped October 5, 1944>
(Sender) Yoshio Kanaya, Yokogawa-cho 1-chome, Hiroshima
(Addressee) Seiji Kanaya, Ikebe Unit, Western Army 8063rd
Division C/O Shimonoseki Post Office

Dear Eldest Brother Seiji,

Has there been any changes since last time? Things are the same as always. I haven't been writing letters as it has been difficult to get any postcards lately.

By the way, the order for mobilization finally came. My class is going to XX Plant at Mitsubishi Heavy Industries Hiroshima. We leave at the end of this month. Up until then, we will have tests every day at school. However I have wrapped a headband around my head and am prepared for the hardest of battles. It has turned autumn and the weather is good. As it is that time of year when they say "horses grow stout under the high sky," I expect to study well, and I will do my best.

Yours Sincerely,

Yoshio

Incidentally, Yoshio mentioned "XX Plant of Mitsubishi Heavy Industries" in the letter, but this was probably a misunderstanding. Yoshio, who was in class 20, would have been mobilized to Toyo Kogyo.

On July 18, amid the deteriorating state of the war, the Tojo Cabinet resigned on mass, and on July 22, the Koiso Cabinet was inaugurated. However, the government's position on the war was unchanged and it declared that the war shall continue. As such, there were no prospects that the war would come to a conclusion.

In October, the Japanese Army responded to the U.S. Army's landing of Leyte Island, by storming into Leyte Bay between October 23 and October 25. However, the Japanese combined fleet was annihilated, and more than half of the large war vessels were lost, including the battleship Musashi. Then in November, the U.S. Army began full-on aerial attacks on the Japanese main islands using B-29 bombers taking off from Guam, Saipan and Tinian Island.

Then the B-29 bombers even came to the Hiroshima district. On November 11 at about 10:15 a.m., a B-29 bomber dropped 12 incendiary bombs in the hills of Harada Village (now Onomichi City) of Mitsugi District. Luckily there was no death toll, just partial burning of village houses. However it was a mystery as to why the U.S. Army had chosen to aerially attack mountain villages in Hiroshima Prefecture, but not aerially attack Hiroshima.

<Letter stamped November 14, 1944>
(Sender) Yoshio Kanaya, Yokogawa-cho 1-chome, Hiroshima
(Addressee) Seiji Kanaya, Sakane Unit, Western Army No. 8063rd Division C/O Shimonoseki Post Office

Dear Eldest Brother Seiji,
The leaves have completely fallen from the trees and it feels very much like winter. Today was really cold. By the way, I trust you are still well. I heard the B-29s came even here the other day, but even if they bombed it's okay. That's because the self-defense force was perfectly laid out.

Father is saying that he will soon be traveling to where you are. If he brings a new fountain pen, please return the one that I brought to you. Be sure to stay well.

Yours sincerely,
Yoshio

After the U.S. military's aerial attacks on the Japanese main islands intensified, it was thought that there would inevitably be large-scale aerial attacks by the United States on the city of Hiroshima, and on November 18 the first stage of forced building evacuation and demolition started. Then, by the end of that year, the first stage of compulsory building evacuation and demolition ended with 400 buildings demolished and 1,029 groups of people and 4,210 individuals evacuated. A succession of subsequent phases of compulsory building evacuation work continued after that as well.

In the home in Yokogawa-cho where Yoshio was living in, life went on with Yoshio, his parents and Hiroshi, who returned home from Etajima Island about once a week. All four members of the family had been living in good health for some time. But then, around autumn that year, Futayo began to get a recurring fever and cough and was leading a life in and out of bed. It was thought that Futayo's condition was a cold at first, but the slight fever and cough continued without improvement. Kiyosuke asked for a diagnosis from Dr. Takeko Hiramatsu, a local town doctor, and she diagnosed bronchitis. For confirmation, a second opinion was sought from another doctor, Dr. Atsuji Takada in Nishihikimido-machi (now Nishitokaichimachi or Hirosemachi, Naka Ward, Hiroshima), but the diagnosis was the same. Kiyosuke decided to allow Futayo to convalesce at home without change. Yet the year drew to a close with Futayo still showing no signs of recovery.

For the New Year, Seiji returned on a temporary leave pass from Mutsure Island but Kiyosuke did not give a detailed explanation to Seiji about Futayo's condition. In his heart, Kiyosuke felt a certain anxiety about Futayo's condition. He had a foreboding that perhaps this was the last time Futayo and Seiji would see each other. However, Kiyosuke was unable to say such an indiscreet thing to Seiji who was engaged in military service.

In the United States meanwhile, the nuclear weapon development project, which had begun its first embryonic movement in August two years earlier, was progressing steadily, and they were striving to make the creation of the atomic bomb a reality at the Los Alamos Laboratory. Moreover, on December 17, the 509th Composite Group was formed. It would be given the task of dropping the atomic bombs on Japan. It would later become the operations group to which belonged the B-29s that would drop the atomic bombs on Hiroshima and Nagasaki.

When the new year came around and it became 1945, Seiji was reassigned from the Shimonoseki Western Army 8063rd Division to the Manchukuo 815th Division and became a paymaster apprentice officer.

Futayo's illness showed no sign of improvement even in January, and in addition to fever and coughing, she began to experience diarrhea. By mid-February, she was unable to get up and just lay in bed. Kiyosuke worked hard to get medicine and he also fed her nutrients such as meat and fish, which he had managed to procure despite the difficulty to come by these things. But soon she was unable to even take in a sufficient amount of food. At 1:00 a.m. on March 9, with Kiyosuke, Hiroshi and Yoshio at her side, Futayo passed away. Directly before dying, she was quite lucid and said words to her family. Then, she breathed her last as if falling asleep. She was 44 years of age when she died. Seiji, who was at his division in Manchukuo, received news of Futayo's death by a telegram sent by Kiyosuke. As Seiji was in military service and unable to come home, all he could do was to pray for his mother's soul on foreign ground.

Futayo's cause of death is thought to have been tuberculosis. There were no drugs that could effectively treat tuberculosis at the time, and as it was also a time when it was not possible to obtain food that provided adequate nutrition, there was nothing that could be done and the illness just progressed unabated.

For Yoshio, who had only just turned 15, his mother's death was immensely sorrowful. Nevertheless, it was not a time when one could forever mourn over one's parent's death. The situation of the war was driving everyone to their wits' end.

Before daybreak on March 10, the day following Futayo's death,

Tokyo was turned into a scene of carnage by large-scale aerial attacks by U.S. bombers. Between 12:07 a.m. and 2:37 a.m. on that day, about 300 B-29 bombers flew over Tokyo very low in the sky, concentrating on Koto Ward, and indiscriminately dropped incendiary bombs. In one night, as many as 100,000 lives were lost.

Having already lost control of the sky and control of the sea, Japan became scorched earth, with not just Tokyo, but nearly all cities inside Japan being attacked by U.S. bombers. However, for some strange reason, several cities, including Hiroshima, had not been aerially attacked. Upon entering March, even Hiroshima was subject to the issuance of warnings and alerts on an almost daily basis. Yet Hiroshima had not received any large-scale air raids.

On March 26, Iwo Jima was taken by the U.S. Army. Iwo Jima is a small island about 8 kilometers east to west and 4 kilometers south to north located in the Ogasawara Islands, about 1,250 kilometers south of Tokyo. In addition to using this island to provide early warning of U.S. bombers flying to bomb the Japanese main islands, the Japanese military used the island as an air force base for interceptor fighters. For the U.S. Army, Iwo Jima was an island that they very much wanted to control to secure an emergency landing base for the B-29 bombers attacking the Japanese main islands from the Marianas Islands and a base for the escort fighters. After unleashing a fierce assault by warship from February 16, which was enough to permanently change the Islands topography, a fully equipped U.S. military commenced landing operation from February 19. In response, about 20,000 soldiers of the Japanese military guard dug a mesh of underground pathways around the island and fiercely defended the island for as long as a month in a fight to the death that finally ended on March 26. As a consequence of Japan losing Iwo Jima, the aerial attacks on the Japanese main islands were escalated in earnest.

On March 19 from 7:20 a.m. onward, one week prior to Japan's defeat at Iwo Jima, about 350 U.S. carrier-based airplanes staged a large aerial attack centered on Kure. On that day, about 7 carrier-based bombers flew to Hiroshima after 9:00 a.m. and although there was machine-gun fire, the city was spared of major damage. That day was the school admission results for Hiroshima First Middle School, and students who had sat the entrance exam and their siblings or parents passed tensely through the city that was sounding aerial attack warnings toward First Middle School to view the announced results.

Yoshio was heartbroken by his mother's death. Although he had experienced the death of his grandparents, this was his first experience of loss from the death of a close blood relative. Although his mother's death was certainly a tragedy for Yoshio, if we consider what was later in store for Yoshio's life, we cannot clearly determine whether or not her death was a misfortune. If Futayo had lived, then perhaps on August 6, both Yoshio and Futayo would have lost their lives to the atomic bomb. Or even in the unlikely event that she survived the blast like Kiyosuke, upon learning the death of Yoshio, Futayo would have suffered a mother's sorrow of losing her son.

On April 7, the Japanese government witnessed the end of the Koiso Cabinet and the Suzuki Cabinet was inaugurated.

<Letter stamped April 6, 1945>
(Sender) Yoshio Kanaya, Yokogawa-cho 1-chome, Hiroshima
(Addressee) Yoshie Furukawa, Goku Otake Town, Saeki District, Hiroshima Prefecture

Dear Big Sister Yoshie,

I received your letter of condolence. Today, already 47 days have flown by since my mother's death. I cannot express in words the sadness and loneliness I feel to have lost my only mother in this world. It's no use feeling regret now, but I feel in my chest the sadness that I did not adequately perform filial duties in the past. I will also follow your advice and keep my mother solely in the world of my dreams.

As today is a factory holiday to save electricity, I took out Mother's diary and I was filled with tears of gratitude at the great love of my mother that was overflowing from every single page. Considering this, I will throw myself into the production that is my duty to comfort the soul of my buried mother.

My lymph glands are not perfect, but I have physically recovered and have been going to the factory since yesterday. I am sorry to have caused you to worry.

The air raids are inevitable. Even if we came under attack, we cannot leave our posts. We are determined to serve our production unit until the end and stay with our machines. We will work together. Until the day of victory. The weather is heating up, so look after yourself.

Yours Sincerely,

Yoshio

April 5, 1945

Yoshie, to whom the letter was addressed, was his cousin living in Otake. She was the daughter of Kiyosuke's younger sister. Since graduating from the Hiroshima Prefectural Hiroshima First Senior Girls High School, she had been working in the women's volunteer corps at the marine corps of Otake. Three years older than Yoshio, she was like a big sister to Yoshio, who had no girls as siblings. Especially since his mother died, Yoshio loved Yoshie like a real older sister, and he presumed on Yoshie's kindness like a real younger brother.

Incidentally, "Mother's diary" mentioned in the letter was not to be found among my grandfather's mementos, and so I think it unfortunately was destroyed in the atomic bomb blast. This letter is all that remains of Yoshio's writings about his mother. Being revealed from the lines of this letter, is a figure desperately wrestling with deep sadness that is quite different from the normally high-spirited Yoshio.

On April 1, the U.S. military began to land on Okinawa. The Japanese military mobilized even civilians to attempt do-or-die resistance against the invading United States. In the evening of April 6, several warships including the battleship Yamato departed from Tokuyama Bay in Yamaguchi Prefecture and headed for Okinawa Island with only enough fuel for a one-way journey. In the afternoon of April 7, the next day, U.S. military carrier-based planes attacked in wave formations and most of the warships were sunk, including the Yamato. Then, the ferocious battle on Okinawa took the lives of hundreds of thousands people including the U.S. military, Japanese military and civilians. The highly organized battle reached a conclusion on June 23.

Meanwhile, in the United States, an event that deeply saddened the American public occurred on April 12. President Truman suddenly died of a stroke. He was 63 years old. As a result, Vice-President Harry Truman was hurriedly made the new President. There is an interesting anecdote that in response to the death of President Roosevelt, Prime Minister Kantaro Suzuki sent an official telegram to the U.S. government

Yoshio as a third-grade middle school student
Provided by Toshinori Kanaya

expressing condolences, despite the United States being an enemy nation.

Having been appointed President, Truman basically carried on Roosevelt's policies. With respect to the Manhattan Project, however, Truman had hardly heard anything about it while he was Vice-President. As a result, initially he did not show a strong interest in the project to develop the atomic bomb. However, he heard from a military advisor that it could take as long as another year and a half for Japan to surrender. Truman, who was serious about minimizing the damage to the men and officers of the U.S. Army, apparently began to then proactively consider dropping the atomic bomb on Japan if it was developed.

While still in deep grief from the experience of his mother's death, Yoshio became a third-grade middle school student. This time, there had hardly been any classes at school, and Yoshio had been continuing working every day with factory labor from dawn to dusk as part of labor mobilization. We can perceive Yoshio's state of mind at that time from a letter that Kiyosuke wrote to Seiji.

<Letter stamped April 21, 1945>
(Sender) Kiyosuke Kanaya, Yokogawa-cho 1-chome, Hiroshima
(Addressee) Seiji Kanaya, Iwamoto Unit, Manchukuo 815th Division, C/O Manchukuo 302nd Military Post Office.

Dear Seiji
I believe you are continuing your hard work in military affairs. We are still all managing fine without any problems. Yoshio is full of energy every day assisting in boosting production of military equipment at the XX Works as part of full-year mobilization. Recently, he's developed quite a body, he says he is a bit more than 163 cm and weighs 56 kg. He is now able to prove himself useful at any time. He has plenty of willingness and he is reliable too.

However, I'm a bit concerned that he has easily enough cheek for his 16 years. Now without his mother, I think I will have to put all my effort into his growing up over the next few years. He needs a warm heart, and I will have a hard time providing that. It would help if you occasionally write a letter too. (Rest of letter omitted.)

According to this letter, Yoshio was 163 centimeters tall and weighed 56 kilograms, which was quite tall for those times. Also even though Kiyosuke was passionate about education, it appears he was not always on Yoshio's back about working hard at school work as well as the labor mobilization. Incidentally, the "16 years" mentioned was counting the number of calendar years and not Yoshio's age, which was 15.

Aerial attacks by B-29 bombers were repeatedly carried out on various cities on the Japanese main islands, and finally, the city of Hiroshima received damage from B-29s. On April 30, 6:55 a.m., the air raid warnings were sounded in Hiroshima, and directly after, a single B-29 bomber flew over and dropped 10 bombs. Many of the bombs were dropped in the vicinity of Chugoku Haiden (now Chugoku Electric Power Company) straight west down the road from the First Middle School front gate, causing building fires. One of bombs that were dropped fell in the vicinity of the entrance on the east side of the First Middle School assembly hall, leaving a 7-meter wide 3-meter deep crater, and causing the ceiling of the chemistry classroom on the east side of the assembly hall to collapse. Although there were fortunately no lives lost in First Middle School, 10 Hiroshima citizens died and 16 were injured.

That day was the first time that Hiroshima had incurred damage from aerial attacks by U.S. bombers. However Kure, which was a Military port, had been insistently incurring aerial attacks by U.S. bombers from spring that year. This caused fear to spread among Hiroshima citizens that a large-scale bombing of Hiroshima would eventually come.

On May 7 in Europe, Germany made an unconditional surrender.

Fellow Axis partner Italy had already surrendered in September 1943. This left Japan, forced to continue waging war as just one country against the countries of the world.

<Letter stamped July 1, 1945>
(Sender) Yoshio Kanaya, Yokogawa-cho 1-chome, Hiroshima
(Addressee) Yoshie Furukawa, Goku Otake Town, Saeki District, Hiroshima Prefecture

Dear Big Sister Yoshie,

It is raining every day, which is no fun. I am writing this letter because our work finished today at 3:30 p.m. and I came home early. I assume you are working every day in good health as usual. I am still doing the same work. I am full of energy. Please rest assured that Father and Hiroshi are also well.

Recently, I have been going to school about once a week to work a 24-hour shift to protect it against aerial attack. The school building may be old, but nevertheless, our school has a proud tradition, and we don't want it to now become prey for U.S. bombers.

Yoshitake of Nagoya visited us while in Hiroshima on business for two days. He appeared to be in as fine health as ever.

Any good news from Otake? Is Mitchan well? Please pass on my regards. It is a public holiday for us tomorrow. I am thinking what to do.

I will write again later. I enjoy receiving letters. Please reply. Please pass on my regards to my uncle and aunt. That's it for today.

Good-bye,
Yoshio.

Although just three months had passed since his mother's death, it appears that Yoshio's old exuberance had returned at this time. Incidentally, from this letter we know that since becoming a third grader, Yoshio had stayed overnight at school about once a week under a 24-hour stay system. It was his appointment to this duty called "air defense personnel" that had decided Yoshio's fate on the morning of August 6.

<Letter stamped July 1, 1945>
(Sender) Yoshio Kanaya, Yokogawa-cho 1-chome, Hiroshima
(Addressee) Yoshie Furukawa, Goku Otake Town, Saeki District, Hiroshima Prefecture

Thank you for going out of your way to visit us the other day. We also immensely appreciated the fine articles you brought with you that time.

Thanks that those, I have been going to the factory full of energy. Concerning the matter of the black canvas shoes that we talked about that time, would it be possible to get a pair? You see, I don't have any shoes and it is hard without them.

If you find a candidate for my wife, a good person, could you ask?

Please don't think bad of me for just sending letters only when my own circumstances are bad.

Good-bye

To big sister Yoshie. From Yoshio.

This letter was written on the same July 1. As the content reveals, middle school students often were impeded by a lack of shoes at that time, and they had to go to school wearing split-toe boots or going barefoot.

In the night of July 1, the day Yoshio sent the letters to Yoshie, from

11:50 p.m. to 2:30 a.m. the next morning, the city of Kure was aerially attacked by about 80 B-29 bombers, and more than half the central area of Kure was burned by incendiary bombs. The air raid took 1,800 lives.

After Kure suffered this immense damage, there were no more large-scale aerial attacks by the U.S. bombers in Hiroshima Prefecture for a while. Already, most of the cities throughout Japan had become charred earth as a result of aerial attacks. Despite this, the Japanese Army, envisaging that the U.S. Army would land on the Japanese main islands and engage in land battle, began to make preparations for a battle on the Japanese main islands. In Hiroshima as well, it was thought that the city would definitely receive a large-scale aerial attack by the U.S. military soon, and air defense systems were being bolstered.

Yoshio, while applying himself to labor mobilization at Toyo Kogyo, was staying overnight in a 24-hour vigil as an air-defense personnel about once a week.

<Letter stamped July 23, 1945>
(Sender) Yoshio Kanaya, Yokogawa-cho 1-chome, Hiroshima
(Addressee) Yoshie Furukawa, Goku Otake Town, Saeki District, Hiroshima Prefecture

Dear Big Sister Yoshie,

Thank you for replying. Your letter came just when I was thinking that you might not answer. Up until now the weather has been cloudy but today the sky was clear.

I was thinking, "Today I will complain about things in my letter." But now the weather is good, I won't.

Please don't say anything cynical. Try to get me some shoes. Please. It'll be a scary outcome if I don't get them.

In addition to that, could I have a stationary knife if you have one? But one with color on it won't do. It would be too embarrassing to use.

By the way, are you well? Pardon, what....? Are you saying it's cheeky to ask? Forgive my manners. I want to say that I am the same as always, but three days ago I got a tummy ache and a fever. The fever was 39.8. It was a real head and tummy ache. I am resting from it today. The cause was that I had just gone loquat picking with 170 First Middle School students mobilized to Toyo Kogyo to a place called the loquat mountain (located in Furuta-mura, Hiroshima). You wouldn't believe how many I ate. I sat in the branches and ate about 150 loquat before eating my meal, and then I ate another 80 afterward. I had a real tummy upset four days later.

Have you gone a tinge black? Stay well won't you. I don't know about holidays in August.

Pass my regards on to everyone. Signing off for today.

Good-bye.

Yoshio.

This letter was Yoshio's final writing that he left to this world. Just two weeks later, Yoshio would leave this world. His parting "good-bye"— or "*sayonara*" which he actually wrote in different kanji as a pun—literally became his farewell message.

On July 24, from 6:00 a.m. onward, 870 carrier aircraft flew in and attacked the city of Kure and Kure Military Port, and the warships anchored there incurred considerable damage from gunfire. But yet, there had not been any large-scale attack on the city of Hiroshima.

On July 25, General Carl Spaatz, commander of the U.S. Strategic Air Forces in the Pacific issued a written order to drop the atomic bomb. In this document, it ordered that, on a date from August 3 onward, an atomic bomb be dropped by visual bombing on either Hiroshima, Kokura, or Nagasaki, decided by weather conditions.

On July 26, the Potsdam Declaration was announced and Prime Minister Suzuki announced in a press conference that "I consider the three-country joint statement (Potsdam Declaration) to be a rehash of the Cairo Conference. As a government, we do not consider it to have important value. We can only ignore it. We can only advance toward a resolved, thorough execution of the war." And he ignored the call for Japan's surrender.

Although it was Japan that rejected the Potsdam Declaration, schemes for peace moves with the Allied Powers had been going on in secret. In these peace moves, numerous attempts had already been made from the end of 1944 onward. However, as peace moves were rejected by the neutral country Soviet Union, which had expressed its intention to participate in the war against Japan at the Yalta Conference held in February, and due to the Japan side's strong insistence of the continuation of the Imperial system as a condition for an armistice, peace was unable to be realized.

On July 28, 6:10 a.m., 950 carrier aircraft and 110 heavy bombers, mostly B-29, of the U.S. Army conducted a repeat aerial gunfire assault on Kure and Kure Military Port. Buildings in the city and the anchored warships incurred considerable damage. On the same day, two of the B-24 bombers that participated in the Kure air raid flew by Hiroshima, and one bomber was shot down by an anti-aircraft gun. The plane crashed in the mountains of Yahata, Itsukaichi-cho, and two crewmen were captured.

August came, and overcast skies hung over Hiroshima from about August 2 as Typhoon No. 8 advanced north in the East China Sea. The weather on August 3 was intermittent rain and strong winds. On August 4, the weather was slowly recovering, but it was still partly sunny, partly overcast. The hot summer days returned on Sunday August 5, under the impact of a high pressure system in the Pacific Ocean.

At 9:20 p.m. on August 5, an alert warning was sounded in

Hiroshima, and then again at 9:27 p.m., an air raid warning was sounded. At 11:55 p.m., the air raid warning was canceled. At 12:25 a.m., the air raid warning was again sounded but later canceled at 2:10 a.m. the same day. Despite the two warnings, the city of Hiroshima, for some reason, did not incur an aerial attack and the morning of August 6 arrived without incident.

On the morning of August 6, Yoshio called out with his usual cheerfulness,

"I'm off now. See you when I get back."

And leaving his home in Yokogawa-cho, Yoshio headed off for school. That day, a Monday, it was Yoshio's turn to be air-defense personnel. He was to stay overnight at the school in a 24-hour shift.

This was Yoshio's final parting from his father.

Chapter 3 Little Boy

August 6, 1945, 6:30 a.m. Japan time.

Inside a long-range B-29 flying at 3,000 meters above the Pacific Ocean, Second Lieutenant Jeppson was alone in a cramped, grease-filled space, busy with his job. Jeppson was the crewman in charge of electric circuit control (bomb assembly and maintenance). He was carefully removing three green plugs fitted to the gigantic bomb housed in the bomb bay and replacing them with red plugs. This process connected the detonating circuit and put the bomb in a state where it could explode at any time.

Earlier, in the wee hours of that day, three B-29s took off from Tinian Island in the Central Pacific Ocean charged with a secret mission. They were heading for the Japanese main islands via Iwo Jima. One of those planes was the Enola Gay, and its mission was to drop a special bomb called Little Boy.

Little Boy was a cylindrical shape, 3 meters in length, 75 centimeters in maximum diameter, and roughly 4 tons in weight. It was a nuclear bomb loaded with uranium 235. However, apart from the pilot and several crew members, no one had been informed about the kind of

Little Boy
Provided by Pacific Press Service

function that this bomb possessed. The bomb's target city was still undecided, with the only criteria being a city in western Japan.

As it was carrying Little Boy, which was heavier than regular bombs, the Enola Gay's bomb bay had been considerably modified with all guns, except the tail gun, and armor plates removed to lighten the fuselage.

Upon finally returning from the bomb bay to the cabin, Jeppson reported the completion of the task to Captain Parsons. Parsons moved to the location of the pilot, Colonel Tibbets, sitting in the cockpit, and reported that the plug replacement was complete. Tibbets turned on the switch of the intercom and announced to all crewmen,

"We are carrying the world's first atomic bomb."

At that moment, surprise and agitation spread throughout the cabin. Most of the crew up until that point had not been told the details of their mission.

The pilot in command of the Enola Gay, Paul Tibbets had been appointed in December 9, 1944, the previous year, as commander of the 509th Composite Group, which was established to conduct atomic bombings. His appointment to the group was of course secret to outside

The Enola Gay crew (Colonel Tibbets is in the center)
Provided by Pacific Press Service

the group, and even inside the group, only Tibbets, the unit commander and a few other people knew their mission was to conduct atomic bombing on Japan. Many of the group personnel, with closed lips, had repeatedly carried out special drills without knowing their mission.

The group initially set up a secret base in Wendover in the state of Utah. After visually dropping a bomb dummy unit using the Norden bombsight as the aiming point to determine the bomb target, the group then directly went ahead with repeatedly conducting drills of sudden 155-degree turns and sudden drops. The drills required an as-accurate-as-possible dropping on the aiming point. As a result of this intensive training, the group developed the capability to drop a dummy bomb within a 100-meter radius.

After moving to Tinian Island in May the following year, the group flew to various cities in Japan and dropped pumpkin-shaped large dummy bombs weighing five tons called pumpkin bombs, using preset aiming points as the target. Then the group then went directly ahead with continuing drills of sudden turns and sudden drops. At that time, the crew began to get the feeling that they must be entrusted with some kind of serious mission. However, they did not know what it was, and they were strictly forbidden to talk about their mission. The crew simply followed orders and silently continued the drills.

* * *

The start of the atomic bomb's development goes back to 1939. At the time, U.S. physicist Leo Szilard, who was worried that Nazi Germany was developing nuclear weapons, wrote a letter to advise the President that the United States must also urgently develop nuclear weapons. After persuading physicist Albert Einstein to add his signature, Szilard sent the letter to President Roosevelt. Roosevelt initially did not show much interest to this advice, but when Germany invaded Poland and The

Second World War broke out, Roosevelt sensed a real threat of Germany developing a nuclear bomb and using it. In 1942, he appointed physicist Robert Oppenheimer to lead the full-scale development of nuclear weapons in what was called the Manhattan Project. This project had proceeded in the utmost secrecy at a laboratory in Los Alamos in the state of New Mexico. The person put in charge of this project was Brigadier General Lesley Groves. Incidentally, among the scientists working on the development under Oppenheimer's lead were quite a few Jewish scientists who had fled the Nazi persecution and had come to the United States from various European countries as refugees.

Three years later in July 16, 1945, the world's first nuclear experiment was conducted, and manufacturing of an atomic bomb got fully underway. These were the uranium-type Little Boy and the plutonium-type Fat Boy (the atomic bomb that was dropped on Nagasaki). Germany had already surrendered on May 7 of that year, and the dropping of the atom bomb on Japan began to be treated as a real possibility. Already on April 27 of that year, the U.S. Military's initial meeting of the Target Committee led by Groves had been held, and the selection criteria in the event that an atomic bomb was dropped on Japan were decided as follows:

a. Consideration is to be given to large urban areas of not less than 3 miles in diameter. And such areas should exist in larger populated areas.
b. The targets should be between the Japanese cities of Tokyo and Nagasaki.
c. The target should have a high strategic value.

Then, over the two days of May 10 to 11, the second meeting of the Target Committee was held, and as a result, the four cities of Kyoto, Hiroshima, Yokohama, and Kokura were selected. The next day on May 12, a command was issued to prohibit the regular bombing of those four cities. This was to preserve the target city so that the degree of destruction of an atomic bomb could be later verified.

On May 28, when the third meeting of the Target Committee was held, the previous mentioned cities of Yokohama and Kokura had been removed, in their place, Niigata had been added. Although Kyoto had been put forward as the target city by Groves, Secretary of War Henry Stimson was vehemently opposed to it on the grounds that Kyoto was the historical and cultural center of Japan and that dropping the bomb on Kyoto could attract hatred from the Japanese people. Thus, Kyoto was removed and Kokura was re-added. Niigata was also later removed on the grounds that the flight distance from Tinian Island was too far. On July 25, in the written directive for the atomic bombing, Hiroshima, Kokura, and Nagasaki were specified as the target cities. It was also decided to proceed with the bombing without notifying Japan beforehand.

The plan at this time was being carried out in top secret, and President Truman, who took office after the sudden death of President Roosevelt on April 12, was accepting of the plan to drop the atomic bomb on Japan.

Before daybreak on July 16, the world's first nuclear test was finally conducted at Alamogordo in the state of New Mexico. At the moment of the explosion, after the brightness of several suns, a fireball appeared at the center, rapidly swelling as it rose, and the surrounding area brightened as if it were midday. Overwhelmed by the direct assault of the thundering noise and blast wave, the many scientists who viewed this explosion from 15 kilometers away at the observation center were dumbfounded by explosive power that was beyond imagination. In no time, the fireball had turned into a mushroom cloud and continued to swell, reaching the stratosphere. Oppenheimer, who attended as one of the scientists, would later recite a verse from Hindu scripture "Now I am become death, a destroyer of worlds."

A report of the nuclear test was immediately sent to President

Truman on July 17, who was in Berlin to attend the Potsdam Conference. This top secret telegram was expressed in the style of a father receiving the news of the birth of a child.

"TO SECRETARY OF WAR FROM HARRISON. DOCTOR HAS JUST RETURNED MOST ENTHUSIASTIC AND CONFIDENT THAT THE LITTLE BOY IS AS HUSKY AS HIS BIG BROTHER. THE LIGHT IN HIS EYES DISCERNIBLE FROM HERE TO HIGHHOLD AND I COULD HAVE HEARD HIS SCREAMS THERE TO MY FARM."

"BIG BROTHER" was referring to the atomic bomb used in the nuclear test at Alamogordo, and "LITTLE BOY" was referring to the planned atomic bomb that would be dropped on Japan. "HIGHHOLD" was Secretary of War Stimson's second home 400 kilometers from Washington, and "MY FARM" referred to the farm owned by the Interim Committee's George Harrison, which was 80 kilometers from Washington. It was meant to describe the size of the explosion as having a flash that could be observed 400 kilometers away and a sound that could be heard 80 kilometers away. From this telegram, it was conveyed that the size of the nuclear explosion was massive.

On July 18, Truman wrote in his diary, "Japs will hold up (surrender) before Russia comes in. I am sure they will when Manhattan appears over their homeland." Truman had already decided to drop the atomic bomb on Japan.

At Potsdam, the three leaders Truman, Churchill and Stalin had met to discuss the handling of Germany's defeat and the handling of Japan after the war. Truman therefore expected the United States would hold an advantageous negotiating position at this conference by playing such a trump card as the dropping of the atomic bomb on Japan. Secretary of State James Byrnes, who accompanied Truman, was particularly considering using it as a strategy against the Soviet Union after Japan's surrender. At that time, Stalin already had received reports of the United

States' nuclear tests from his intelligence operatives, so when Stalin was told this news from Truman, he expressed his congratulations concerning the success of the nuclear tests and replied that he hoped that it could be used effectively against the Japanese, but, of course, his words were nothing but diplomatic flattery.

On July 25, General Spaatz, in command of the U.S. Strategic Air Forces, signed a directive to conduct the atomic bombing. The written orders were to drop an atomic bomb on or after August 3 by visual bombing on one city, Hiroshima, Kokura, or Nagasaki, to be decided by weather conditions.

Considering that on August 3, Typhoon No. 8, which had formed near Iwo Jima on July 16, was heading north in the East China Sea and causing unsettled weather over western Japan, it was decided to wait for the typhoon to pass and conduct the bombing on August 6. The final decision as to which city to bomb was made based on the weather conditions of the three cities on August 6.

On August 6, at 1:45 a.m. Japan time, the Enola Gay loaded with Little Boy took off from Northern Air Strip on Tinian Island. Taking off immediately after were two B-29 bombers accompanying the Enola Gay, the Great Artiste and No. 91 (the Necessary Evil). The planes headed for the Japanese main islands via the sky above Iwo Jima. One hour before the Enola Gay took off, three B-29 bombers had taken off to perform weather reconnaissance of the target candidate cities. The Straight Flush was headed for Hiroshima, the Jabbit III was headed for Kokura, and the Full House was headed for Nagasaki. Ultimately, the reports from the meteorological equipment from the three aircraft would determine which city to drop the atomic bomb on.

* * *

After announcing to the Enola Gay crew that their mission was to drop the atomic bomb, he persuaded himself afresh that loyally executing this mission was the mission given to him as a soldier.

From the intercom, Tibbets announced,

"When the bomb is dropped, Lieutenant Beser will record our reactions to what we see. This recording is being made for history. Watch your language and don't clutter up the intercom."

At 6:40 a.m., the Enola Gay approached the Japanese main islands, and began to increase its altitude. Then, while they were flying over Shikoku, a Japanese fighter plane suddenly approached from the west. Apprehension spread throughout the cabin. As all the Enola Gay's guns except the tail gun had been removed, they would not be able to sufficiently respond to an attack by the fighter, and as the armor plating had also been removed, there was a risk of being shot down if they came under fire and were hit. The plugs that were fitted to the loaded Little Boy had already been switched to the red plugs, and the circuits had been activated, and so if Little Boy was dropped, the chances of it causing a nuclear explosion were high.

The Japanese fighter that had caught the Enola Gay opened fire while in pursuit, but fortunately for the Enola Gay, it was not hit and soon the fighter had drifted away. A mood of relief spread throughout the cabin.

Meanwhile, the weather reconnaissance plane the Straight Flush that had taken off in the direction of Japanese main islands one hour earlier than the Enola Gay, arrived above Hiroshima at 7:09 a.m. At that time, a gap in the clouds was just opening up above Hiroshima and it was possible to see the city of Hiroshima spread out below. It met the permissible weather criteria for dropping Little Boy. Also at that time, the other two weather reconnaissance planes had confirmed the above-sky weather in Nagasaki and Kokura. According to those reports, Kokura had numerous clouds in the sky above and visibility was poor, while the sky was clear above Nagasaki.

At 7:25 a.m., Private Nelson, the Enola Gay's radio operator received "Y3Q3B2C1" as the encoded message from the Straight Flush. It was decoded to the following statement:

"Cloud cover less than 3/10ths at all altitudes. Advice: bomb primary."

With regard to the decision as to which city to make the target for Little Boy, Hiroshima was provisionally made the primary target, Kokura was made the second target, and Nagasaki was made the third target. Later, the final decision would be made based on the weather conditions. Based on reports of the weather reconnaissance planes, Nagasaki had a clear sky, and it was the most ideal for visual bombing. But as Hiroshima was previously decided as the primary target provided that the conditions were acceptable, Hiroshima's fate was sealed at this moment.

The pilot, Colonel Tibbets, after reading the deciphered message, flicked the intercom switch,

"It's Hiroshima."

Then Private Nelson wired the following one-word message to Major Uanna, who was waiting for the message at the forward command base at Iwo Jima:

"Primary."

The Enola Gay rose to an altitude of 9,400 meters and settled into level flight. Trailing behind the Enola Gay, were the two aircraft, the Great Artiste and No. 91 (the Necessary Evil).

At 8:05 a.m., the navigator Captain Van Kirk announced,

"Ten minutes to AP [aiming point]."

Still maintaining altitude, the Enola Gay passed Shikoku, and heading northward over the Seto Inland Sea, it gradually began taking a path to the west. Second Lieutenant Jeppson kept his eyes fixed on the instruments monitoring the electrical circuit of Little Boy. At this stage, they could not afford an abnormality to occur with the electrical circuit controlling Little Boy.

At 8:12 a.m., Van Kirk relayed to Tibbets via the intercom, "IP [initial point]."

After passing directly over the city of Mihara, at 34 degrees 24 minutes north, 133 degrees 5 minutes 30 seconds east, which was the decided initial point, the Enola Gay, which had entered the bombing run, flew toward the aiming point using manual controls. Down below, a range of mountains and areas of houses could be seen, while on the sea's surface, numerous ships were visible.

Using the intercom, Tibbets instructed all the crew, "On glasses."

Before attaching his protective goggles, the co-pilot Captain Lewis wrote,

"There will be a short intermission while we bomb our target."

In order to execute a dropping of Little Boy to accurately hit the aiming point that was set ahead of the Enola Gay, the bombardier would operate the flight course of the aircraft using the Norden bombsight. The Enola Gay's controls switched hands from the pilot Tibbets to the bombardier Major Ferebee.

Soon they would be directly above the city of Hiroshima, yet there was no attack from the Japanese military. They had been pursued by a Japanese fighter once while flying over Shikoku, but after that, they had not encountered any Japanese fighters, nor had there been any anti-aircraft fire from the ground.

At 8:14:30 a.m., the bombardier, Ferebee, while peering in the finder, shouted out that the city center of Hiroshima had entered view. Looking down, they could see the city center of Hiroshima dissected by the tributaries of the Ota River. There was not even a single fire from anti-aircraft guns from the ground.

Ferebee kept his eye focused on the finder, 063096 on the Norden bombsight, the decided aiming point for the bomb, came into sight; it was the distinctive T-shaped Aioi Bridge.

U.S. military aerial photograph of Hiroshima city before dropping the atomic bomb (The T-shaped bridge is Aioi Bridge. Hiroshima First Middle School is about 1 kilometer south east from Aioi Bridge)
Provided by United States National Archives Collection Aerial Photos – Japan Map Center

"I've got it."

Ferebee quickly input the flight speed, altitude, and distance from the aiming point into the Norden bombsight and turned on the signaling tone switch. The signal tone was received by Little Boy. This activated the automatic timing device that was set to cause the bomb to drop down to directly above Aioi Bridge, the decided aiming point. There were no more human operations that needed to be performed; at the given time, the bomb bay would open and Little Boy would drop, and after 43 seconds, it was meant to explode in the sky above the aiming point, Aioi Bridge.

Trailing the Enola Gay by 1.6 kilometers was the Great Artiste. It entered a state of waiting for the moment that Little Boy was dropped to drop three parachutes with measurement wireless systems for studying the conditions at the time of the blast. Trailing 3.2 kilometers behind was No. 91 (the Necessary Evil), which was beginning to make a 90-degree turn to the left to take a photo at the time of the blast.

At 8:15:17 a.m., at the same time the Enola Gay's bomb bay opened, Little Boy was released from the fuselage. As the Enola Gay became about four ton lighter at that moment, the fuselage jumped up about three meters. Little Boy was released from the fuselage. For a split second, it appeared to stay motionless in midair, but in a flash, it began falling toward the ground, forever accelerating.

Ferebee, sitting in the bombardier's seat at the very tip of the nose, looked down from the windshield and yelled out,

"Bomb away."

Immediately, Tibbets turned 155 degrees to the right and descended rapidly to begin retreating from the sky above Hiroshima at full speed. The Great Artiste, having already dropped the three parachutes, made a sharp turn to the left and began to retreat.

Tibbets asked the tail gunner Sergeant Caron over the intercom whether he could see anything. Caron replied that he couldn't see anything.

The time passed slowly, a second at a time. Total silence spread throughout the cabin.

At exactly 8:16 a.m., 43 seconds after being dropped, Little Boy exploded about 600 meters above Shima Hospital some 250 meters south east of the aiming point, Aioi Bridge.

At that moment, the crew inside the Enola Gay, which had retreated to about 17 kilometers away in the north-east sky, experienced a fierce flash that spread throughout the cabin. No one spoke. Tibbets experienced tasting the light inside his mouth during the moment of the flash. He said it was like tasting lead.

The crewman who first gazed upon the frightful spectacle that accompanied the flash was tail gunner Caron. He was sitting in the tail gunner's seat looking toward Hiroshima, which was getting further and further away at maximum speed. Following after the fierce flash, he saw a gigantic spherical mass of air, exploding outward and coming toward the Enola Gay at the speed of sound. Caron tried to give a warning by the intercom, but gripped with fear, he couldn't speak. Just as he gathered his wits and was about to shout, the Enola Gay was assailed by a shock wave, causing the fuselage to jump up.

Then after 4 seconds, Caron shouted at the intercom,

"There's another one coming ! "

The second wave lifted up the Enola Gay again, the radio operator Private Nelson was almost thrown from his seat, and the radar operator Sergeant Stiborik hit the floor.

Tibbets instinctively shouted,

"Flack [we're under fire]!"

Suddenly, there was turmoil in the cabin, but Tibbets quickly comprehended the situation and told the rest of the crew that it was not anti-aircraft fire but a shock wave from the bomb.

Then after the shock wave passed, the turmoil in the cabin gradually returned to calm.

Caron in the tail gunner seat soon settled down again and began taking photos aimed toward the city of Hiroshima, as per his orders. Tibbets commanded Beser to begin recording the impressions from each of the crew.

The Enola Gay first flew at full speed away from Hiroshima directly after Little Boy exploded, but then it turned around and flew over Hiroshima again. It circled the site three times from an altitude of 9,000 meters to observe the state of damage of Hiroshima's city center and take photos.

However, from the sky above Hiroshima, it was not possible to observe the city center as it was covered by the massive mushroom cloud rising up. Nevertheless, there was no mistaking that the city of Hiroshima had been destroyed.

Concerning the state of Hiroshima directly after the dropping of the atomic bomb, crewman Caron wrote the following:

"A column of smoke is rising fast. It has a fiery red core. A bubbling mass, purple gray in color, with that red core. It's all turbulent. Fires are springing up everywhere, like flames shooting out of a huge bed of coals. I am starting to count the fires. One, two, three, four, five, six . . . fourteen, fifteen . . . it's impossible. Here it comes, the mushroom shape that Captain Parsons spoke about. It's coming this way. It's like a mass of bubbling molasses. The mushroom is spreading out. It's maybe a mile or two wide and half a mile high. It's growing up and up and up. It's nearly level with us and climbing. It's very black, but there is a purplish tint to the cloud. The base of the mushroom looks like a heavy undercast that is shot through with flames. The city must be below that. The flames and smoke are billowing out, whirling out into the foothills. The hills are disappearing under the smoke. All I can see now of the city is the main dock and what looks like an airfield. That is still visible. There are planes down there."

Captain Parsons ordered Private Nelson to send a telegram to the

509th Squadron Operations Room on the base at Tinian Island to report that the dropping of Little Boy was a success.

"CLEAR CUT. SUCCESSFUL IN ALL RESPECTS. VISIBLE EFFECTS GREATER THAN ALAMOGORDO. CONDITIONS NORMAL IN AIRPLANE FOLLOWING DELIVERY. PROCEEDING TO BASE."

Mushroom cloud
Provided by Pacific Press Service

At the operations room on Tinian Island, when this message was received and announced to all that were waiting, there was unanimous cheering. Everyone then began hurriedly preparing a celebration in honor of the achievement.

Mess Officer Perry shouted to those around him,

"The Party's on !"

Hiroshima directly after the dropping of the atomic bomb
Provided by Bettmann / CORBIS / amanaimages

The mess crew began busily preparing several hundred pies for a pie-eating competition, boxes of cold beer and lemonade, thousands of hot dogs, beef and salami sandwiches, salads and the like.

Perry sat himself in front of a typewriter in high spirits and began typing out a program for the celebration.

"509TH

FREE BEER PARTY TODAY 2 P.M.

TODAY–TODAY–TODAY–TODAY–TODAY

PLACE–509TH BALL DIAMOND

FOR ALL MEN OF THE 509TH COMPOSITE GROUP

FOUR (4) BOTTLES of BEER PER MAN–NO RATION CARD NEEDED

LEMONADE FOR THOSE WHO DO NOT CARE FOR BEER

ALL-STAR SOFT BALL GAME 2 P.M.

JITTER BUG CONTEST

HOT MUSIC

SURPRISE CONTEST–YOU'LL FIND OUT

Extra-ADDED ATTRACTION, BLONDE, VIVACIOUS, CURVACIOUS, STARLET DIRECT FROM ???????

PRIZES–GOOD ONES TOO

FOOD GALORE BY PERRY & CO. CATERERS

SPECIAL MOVIE WILL FOLLOW AT 1930, "IT'S A PLEASURE" IN

TECHNICOLOR WITH SONJA HENIE

AND MICHAEL O'SHEA"

The Enola Gay returned to the airbase on Tinian Island together with the two aircraft that had accompanied it. The time was 2:58 p.m. Tinian local time or 1:58 p.m. Japan time.

As the crew had left North Field airstrip at 2:45 a.m. Tinian local time, they were utterly exhausted from the roughly 12 hour flight. Nevertheless, upon alighting from the aircraft, they were surrounded by the cheers of close to one thousand soldiers and base personnel and given a warm welcome. General Spaatz immediately awarded the pilot Colonel Tibbets, who executed the mission, with the Distinguished Service Cross, and the other crewmen with the Silver Star.

Then after Tibbets and the crew gave interviews to numerous members of the press, and delivered a two-hour report of their mission, they were finally able to get some rest and sleep.

At about this time, the party was reaching its crest of cheering and excitement. Most of them were soldiers on duty at the base. Meanwhile, the onsite scientists, led by nuclear physicist Philip Morrison, did not attend this party. Although they played a part in the manufacture of the atomic bomb as scientists under the Manhattan Project, the frightful destructive power of the atomic bomb had become reality, and considering the immense number of people who died, as individual people, they were not in a mood to put these realities aside and celebrate.

The news that an atomic bomb was dropped on Hiroshima reached Truman on August 7, the next day. Truman at that time had finished the Potsdam Conference and was about to take lunch at the Officers' dining room on the USS Augusta while returning home over the Atlantic. He received the telegram just as he was about to begin his meal. The message stated that an atomic bomb had been dropped on the city of Hiroshima, that the result was a success, and that it made a greater impact than was measured at the time of the test. And on the map of Japan that accompanied the telegram, the city of Hiroshima was marked by a red circle. This red circle indicated that some tens of hours earlier, this city was struck by a nuclear bomb.

Truman rose from his chair, tapped his fork on his glass, and once he had caught the attention of those around him, he announced the success of the atomic bomb. At that moment, there was a cheer throughout the room.

The next day after returning to the United States, President Truman gave a radio address. He announced the successful dropping of an atomic bomb on Japan and he said the following:

"We have spent two billion dollars on the greatest scientific gamble in history — and won."

Chapter 4 August 6, 1945, Hiroshima

Like any typical year in Hiroshima, the summer of 1945 had continuing hot days. However, on August 3 and 4, Typhoon No. 8 had passed northward over the East China Sea and had hit landfall at the Korean Peninsula, causing rainy and very windy weather. During those two days, the heat subsided to temperatures easier to cope with. However on the Sunday of August 5, the sky cleared, and the hot summer once again returned.

On the morning of the sixth, Yoshio left his home in Yokogawa-cho and set off for school. It was his turn to be on air-defense personnel duty from that day until tomorrow morning. On that day, a total of six third graders, including Yoshio, went to the school for air-defense personnel duty.

The mission of the air-defense personnel was to defend the school from air raids by U.S. bombers. It was organized so that teachers and students, mostly third graders, would take 24-hour shifts. The students assigned to air-defense personnel duties were chosen from third graders who lived within 30 minutes of the school, and each participating student worked about one shift every week. After the students starting duty replaced the students who did the previous shift at 7:00 a.m., they would carry out duties such as patrolling the school. In the middle of the night, students would form teams of two and take turns being on night watch for one-hour intervals.

At the time, as all students at Hiroshima First Middle School other than the first graders had been mobilized for student labor, the students attending school were the first graders and the third graders on duty for air-defense personnel. The fifth graders were had been mobilized to Toyo Kogyo (now Mazda), and the fourth graders were at the Jigozen Factory of Asahi Seisakujo (Jigozen, Hatsukaichi). Of the third graders, the classes 31, 32, and 33 were at Toyo Kogyo, class 34 was at Kansai Kosakujo, and class 35 was at Hiroshima Airline Company. The second graders had been mobilized to either Jigozen Factory of Asahi Seisakujo or Hiroshima

Airline Company.

Moreover, on that very day, the third graders were given a special mobilization order for the sixth forced building evacuation and demolition, which had started on July 23. This demolition work was allocated as follows. Group B consisting of classes 31, 32, and 33 were working around Tsurumibashi (from Higashihiratsuka-cho to Tsurumi-cho, Naka Ward, Hiroshima; group A were at Toyo Kogyo), and class 35 was working around Dobashi (Sakai-machi, Naka Ward, Hiroshima).

The war had already reduced Japan to catastrophic circumstances. Large-scale air raids had been conducted on numerous cities across Japan from about spring of that year, turning these cities into scorched earth and causing massive damage. Meanwhile, for some reason, Hiroshima had not suffered any assault from U.S. bombers on a scale large enough to be called an air raid. The fact there had not been a large-scale air raid on Hiroshima—a city known as the military capital—left the citizens in constant anxiety about an air raid, and it also caused various conjectures.

For example, perhaps it was because Hiroshima Prefecture was an immigrant prefecture, and there were many people of second generation Japanese-descent in the United States, or perhaps it was because of the number of U.S. prisoners-of-war in Hiroshima. People embraced the conjectures that made the most sense and tried to put each other's minds at rest.

Nevertheless, inside Hiroshima, there had been warnings and alerts issued on nearly a daily basis since around March. Many people found this an unbearable strain to the nerves. It was both physically and mentally exhausting. From the beginning of August, the following warnings were issued:

Aug. 1: Warning and alert issued at 9:06 p.m. Air-raid warning issued at 9:12 p.m. Air-raid warning lifted at 10:02 p.m. Warning and alert lifted at 10:15 p.m. Warning and alert issued at 11:01 p.m. Air-raid warning issued at 11:22 p.m.

Aug. 2: Air-raid warning lifted at 12:12 a.m. Warning and alert lifted at 12:17 a.m.

Aug. 3: No aircraft came, perhaps due to the effect of the Typhoon.

Aug. 4: Warning and alert issued at 11:50 p.m.

Aug. 5: Warning and alert lifted at 12:35 p.m.

As can be seen, the times of day when these warnings were issued were all after 9:00 p.m., and this tendency was the same for July as well.

The citizens of Hiroshima grew increasingly exhausted from the seemingly daily warnings in the middle of the night. Moreover, as no bombs were actually dropped, even when B-29s flew over, there were many people who stopped feeling a sense of danger when the warnings were issued. Rather than evacuating to an air-raid shelter, many chose to stay sleeping in their homes, saying that today also was another B-29 regular flight.

Upon entering August, it was only the 3rd that, maybe due to the typhoon, did not have air-raid warnings issued during the night-time. From the 4th onward, again the warnings were issued as if they were a nightly occurrence. First, on the 5th, a warning and alert issued at 9:20 p.m. was followed by an air-raid warning issued at 9:27 p.m. That night, as the new moon was close, only the stars were visible in the moonless night sky. The unsettling sound of the air-raid warning siren rang out across this dark sky. At First Middle School as well, the students and teachers serving as air-defense personnel were poised in readiness for an air raid by B-29s. They spent time tensely for a while, but two-and-a-half hours later at 11:55 p.m., the air-raid warning was lifted and they all heaved a sigh of relief.

At that time, the U.S. aircraft that flew over was the B-29 weather reconnaissance plane of the 509th Composite Group that had taken off

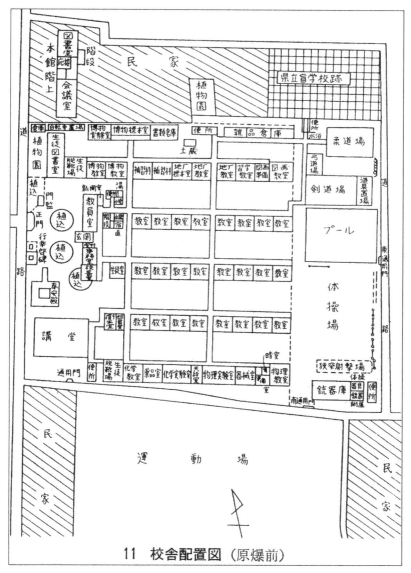

11 校舎配置図 （原爆前）

Sketched layout of First Middle School buildings
Provided by Hiroshima First Middle School Alumni Association

from Tinian Island. That B-29 flying over Hiroshima had reported it would be fair weather for Hiroshima on the upcoming August 6.

Following the lifting of the air-raid alert, the students and teachers serving as air-defense personnel were able to breathe easily for a brief period until an air-raid warning was again issued at 12:25 a.m. Inside the school, the mood once more grew tense, but fortunately, no air raid came and the air-raid warning was lifted at 2:10 a.m. Having had two air-raid warnings during the humid and hot night, the teachers and students had been unable to catch any sleep all night.

At 6:30 a.m., the air-defense personnel were facing the morning fatigued and sleepless from the repeated strain. As the sunrise was 5:24 a.m., the daybreak had completely dispelled the night. It was a quiet morning.

(We are carrying the world's first atomic bomb.)

At 7:09 a.m., another air-raid warning was issued. The radio reported that "Four enemy B-29s were circling above the sky north east of Hiroshima." However the warning was lifted at 7:31 a.m. There was actually just one B-29 flying over the sky above Hiroshima at that time: a plane on weather reconnaissance called the Straight Flush.

After the air-raid warning was lifted, Yoshio had arrived at school. When entering the school building, he looked up with squinty eyes at the sky, glaring from the morning sun.

There were several clouds in the sky, but the summer blue sky was expanding and the sun's rays were strong. Today was looking like it would become another hot day.

(Cloud cover less than 3/10ths at all altitudes. Advice: bomb primary.)

It was soon 7:30 a.m. The city was already bustling with the hurried activities of people.

(It's Hiroshima.)

The news could be heard from a radio somewhere that there were "no enemy aircraft above the skies of Chugoku Military District [including Hiroshima]."

Meanwhile, at that moment, an inspector at the Prefectural Police Headquarters located in City Hall received a phone call from Superintendent Teraoka of the Police Defense Department. The sound of a U.S. plane could be heard in the sky above Hiroshima, and so despite the lifting of the warning and alert, the inspector received instructions to not ignore the warning.

At that moment inside the school grounds of First Middle School, roughly 300 first graders, who had come to school by 7:30 a.m., were assembled on the exercise ground on the east side of the school grounds for roll call. Although the assembled students were junior high students, their appearance was odd-looking. Despite being dressed in school uniforms, they were mostly wearing split-toe boots or Japanese sandals for footwear. Only a very few of the students were wearing school shoes. On their heads, they were wearing either air-raid hoods or field caps, on their backs were rucksacks, and in their hands were bamboo brooms, shovels and hoes. The first graders had come to school that day dressed like this because they were to assist in the forced building evacuation and demolition.

After the roll call, the first graders were divided up into two groups. The odd-numbered classes 11, 13, and 15 were to begin working for the forced building evacuation and demolition work just south of the school in the area at the back of City Hall. The even-numbered classes 12, 14, and 16 were to wait in the classrooms until it was time to replace the odd-numbered classes when their work ended.

The third graders who had come to school to perform duties as air defense personnel took over from the third graders who had been performing these duties since the previous day. Up until the time when the first graders assembled, it had been decided that they would tend the sweet potato field that was being cultivated at one end of the sports ground at the south of the school.

At that moment, apart from the seven teachers and the 15-or-so third graders serving as air-defense personnel, there were only the about-150 first graders of the even-numbered classes inside the school grounds. The first graders of the odd numbered classes had departed to perform the forced building evacuation and demolition work at the back of City Hall. Most of the school's other students had been placed in factories as part of the labor mobilization or were performing forced building evacuation and demolition work inside the city. As that particular day was the day of the Sixth Forced Building Evacuation and Demolition, most of Yoshio's fellow third graders had either been mobilized to the forced building evacuation and demolition work around Tsurumibashi and around Dobashi, or mobilized as part of the student labor mobilization to Toyo Kogyo and Kansai Kosakujo.

At 8:05 a.m., the rays of the summer sun were already hot. The temperature had risen to 27 degrees Celsius and humidity was 80%. Today was looking like being another hot and humid day.

(Ten minutes to AP.)

At 8:06 a.m., two large enemy airplanes were observed flying northwest over Matsunaga Observation Post (Matsunaga, Fukuyama). Then, three minutes later at 8:09 a.m., the same observation post reported a correction that there were three airplanes, and this information was passed to the Chugoku Military Headquarters. Upon receiving this message, the Air-Defense Strategy Office of the Chugoku Military Headquarters urgently contacted the Hiroshima Central Broadcasting Bureau (Nobori-cho, Naka Ward, Hiroshima) to issue a warning and alert.

(On glasses.)

At the information liaison office of the Hiroshima Central Broadcasting Bureau received the urgent message from Military Headquarters and when announcer Masanobu Furuta received the written note: "8:13 a.m. Chugoku Military District Information. Three enemy large airplanes. Passing above Saijo heading west. Serious warning is necessary." He rushed into the studio and headed for the broadcast microphone.

At 8:14 a.m., the Nakano Floodlight Station (Nakano-cho, Aki Ward, Hiroshima) heard the roar of large aircraft in the Saijo direction.

At 8:14:30 a.m., the roar of a B-29 reverberated across the sky above the city of Hiroshima.

(I've got it.)

At that moment, in the school grounds of First Middle School, the first graders of the even-numbered classes, who were waiting inside the classroom, began to get rowdy. There had been a harmonious atmosphere among the students of the even-numbered classes during the waiting time until they were to take over working, with some writing out the new timetable, some talking, and others studying or reading books. However someone had noticed the roar in the sky above and had yelled that it was a B-29. Hearing this, some students popped their heads out of the windows and looked up at the sky, while others began running out of the classroom into the school yard. There were also students, who thought it was a B-29 on a routine flight and remained unconcerned with their head down at their desk.

The third graders who had started air defense personnel duties from that morning had left the school grounds and were walking toward the sports ground at the south of the school to begin tending the sweet potato field.

Just at that moment, outside the school wall facing the sports ground, about-350 Hiroshima Girls Senior High students were lining up along the wall to begin cleaning up after the forced building evacuation and demolition that was to take place.

(Bomb away.)

Yoshio, who was outside the school, noticed the roar of the B-29 reverberating across the sky. Squinting over his spectacles, he looked up at the glaring sky. Yoshio, like other citizens of Hiroshima, did not feel that afraid of the B-29 flying high in the sky. Although he had lost sight of the B-29 as it had fallen in the shadow of a building, Yoshio noticed that its flight path was different from usual. Its roar reverberating across the sky sounded like it was turning suddenly at full speed. Then high up in the sky where Yoshio was looking, three parachutes were slowly falling, heading in a north direction while flowing in the wind.

"Parachutes from a B-29?"

Being knowledgeable about aircraft, this suddenly gave Yoshimi an uneasy feel. This was the first time a B-29 had dropped parachutes or the like.

"I wonder why they dropping parachutes . . ."

At that moment, while gazing at the slowly falling parachutes high in the sky and feeling that something was not right, an incredibly powerful flash of light, like a gigantic flashbulb had gone off in front of his eyes, shone all around him, and he lost consciousness.

At Hiroshima Broadcasting Station, the announcer Furuta spoke into the microphone,

"8:13 a.m. Chugoku Military District Information Three enemy large airplanes. Passing above Saijo . . ."

The moment he began reading, Furuta's body was lifted up into space due to a violent impact, and he crashed onto the floor, losing conscious.

Following the flash of an immensity not seeming to belong in this world, the heat rays and bomb blast struck the city of Hiroshima. Immediately after, the entire city suddenly was engulfed in eerie silence and darkness. The period of silence was as long as a few minutes. During those moments, it was a world absent of sound or light, as if the world had ended.

In that short while of silence and darkness, a world appeared that was different from anything until then. This was a world that brought about an unbelievable transformation.

Directly before this ferocious impact, the city of Hiroshima had been bathed in mid-summer sun and full of various everyday sounds and light.

A tram crowded with passengers travelled down the main street, its wheels reverberating noisily. People rushing to work were busily coming and going, and an ox pulling a cart laden with heavy boxes was walking in amongst them. The voices of people could be heard coming from inside houses. Here and there were the crying of babies and the barking of dogs. The people working up a sweat on the forced building evacuation and demolition could be heard laboring away amid a shouting of orders. People from all walks of life had started facing the Monday morning, getting on with their respective daily lives. It may have been the middle of a war, but the city was still abuzz, full of the living energy of people and other living creatures.

This everyday raucous on the streets had in a split second vanished from this world. Then, the first sounds that could be heard breaking the silence, amid this blackness, were people's cries of anguish. At first, they could be heard faintly from here and there, but steadily, the cries completely filled the entire city until they were ringing out as if the earth itself was trembling.

Then, like a fog lifting, the darkness became incrementally lighter. It became clear that the majority of cries were coming from beneath the collapsed buildings. But feint moans could also be heard from the mouths of those on the street, strewn about as if they had been knocked over where they were standing.

Accompanying the people's cries ringing out like they were the trembling earth itself, an eerie landscape was appearing. Everything that had existed up until now in the city of Hiroshima had been smashed to pieces and indiscriminately scattered everywhere.

Many people had fallen to the ground. Most of them were already dead. They had various shapes and appearances. Some people were fully charred black with their bodies folded like prawns. Others had their limbs torn off, leaving just head and torso. There were also many people with their insides protruding from their abdomens. A pregnant woman had fallen alone, her abdomen was massively torn and her uterus had come out all swollen. The fetus had rolled a short distance from the woman. The firefighting tanks, which had been installed here and there around the city, were covered with corpses. It was as if many people, spotting a single water tank, had dived into it, vying to be first, and had died with their heads stuck in the water. In the gutters of the streets as well, people had died upside down with just their lower limbs showing as if they had dived head first in a rush decision to try to shield their bodies. There were women who were face down motionless, as if they had been trying to protect their babies. A soldier, nearly totally naked had fallen gripping only his weapon. Both eyes were wide open, and from his mouth and nose, blackened blood had flowed out. It was as if all of them were acting out every single possible form that a human corpse could take. Such ghastly states were not limited to people either. A military horse was galloping away while flames streamed from its burning back. An ox, still tethered to a cart lay on the road with its insides protruding from its abdomen, writhing with its hind legs continuously kicking. All the life that had breathed in this city up until just previously had been almost entirely extinguished.

Inside this scene, most of the people struggling to hang on to life looked more like cooked lumps of flesh than human beings. For most of them, their clothes had been blown away and they were naked. Moreover, their bodies were fully covered in horrific burns. Their hair had been frizzed by the heat rays, and their skin, cooked by full-body burns, was hanging flayed from the body like dirty ripped clothes.

On the surface of their bodies where the skin had peeled away, reddish brown membrane lay exposed from which blood and bodily fluid oozed and dropped. Most of the people had a vacant stare and were in a state of stunned shock. Meanwhile, a mother cradling a blood-covered baby was wandering around shouting out things as if she had lost her mind. Elsewhere, an infant was crying and screaming out groping at the bosom of her mother, who was already dead.

As the world of darkness that had engulfed the entire city gradually became lighter, fires then began to flare up all over the place. These flare ups immediately blazed and gigantic flames and black clouds spiraled up. Ferocious twisters began to occur. As a result, the entire city was soon in flames.

With the city enveloped in flames, it was like the sky was burning up. Inside the school grounds of First Middle School, where Yoshio was, it was of course no exception. It was yet another corner of this transformed world.

When Little Boy dropped, the students in the school were wary about the fact that, despite the lifting of the warning, there was a roar reverberating in the sky. But most didn't consider that they could be injured by the bomb. The main building and lecture hall of the First Middle School building were two stories high, but all the classrooms were located in an old one-story wooden building. The moment Little Boy exploded, most of the first graders waiting inside the classroom had no means to defend themselves when the building crashed down on top of them.

Little Boy exploded, and after the heat rays and bomb blast flattened the school building, all was shut into a world of darkness. After a while, amid this darkness, only the sun could be seen vaguely up in the completely dark sky like a full moon.

Then after the prolonged eerie silence, the voices of students began to be heard from here and there, buried under the collapsed school building. Most of these were close to screams.

"Mom!"

"Damn it! What the hell!"

"Long live the Emperor!"

"Aah! It hurts!"

"Help me!"

"Long live First Middle School!"

Among them, lying there crushed, there were some students who began chanting the Imperial Rescript to Soldiers and Sailors; there were some who sang the Japanese national anthem; and there were some who sang the First Middle School fight song Evening of Carp Castle.

There were students who, in frantic desperation, managed to free themselves from the collapsed building, and many of those were injured. There were students who, after escaping the building, had earnestly tried to stop blood gushing from their arms and legs by wrapping these wounds with their socks. However, for most of the students, even though they had escaped the building, they were unable to stand. They just lay there, where they were.

Many students tried their hardest to help their classmates still trapped under the building. But they themselves were suffering from horrendous burns and cuts. Then most of them began to experience strange swelling on their heads. They were like dark reddish spheres. The eyes and mouths of their faces became like slits barely able to open. Their clothes were blown away in the fierce bomb blast, and there were students who were close to naked. With burns all over their bodies, the student's skin on their hands and feet peeled away until it was left dangling from the roots of their nails, giving the illusion that they had dirty rags hanging from their bodies. There were already students who had perished where they were, crushed under the school building. It wasn't long before fires began to flare up from various places of the collapsed building and the building became engulfed in flames.

In addition to the first graders and the third graders, the other people in the school were the school principal Toyoichi Watanabe and numerous teachers and other staff members inside the main building. They had been buried under the building and were unable to escape. Even if they had escaped, their injuries had been severe.

When Yoshio, who had fallen unconscious in the moment of the violent flash, came to in a hazy state of consciousness, the world was dark all around him. Yoshio had no idea where he was. He thought something must have happened, but had no idea what. It also seemed like he was hearing screaming voices around him. But he was unable to move his body at all. Yoshio fell unconscious again.

The school wall that faced the sports ground that Yoshio had been heading toward had collapsed all at once. When this happened, the Hiroshima Girls Senior High students lined up on the outside of the wall had mostly been buried under the collapsed wall. Parts of the girls' arms and legs underneath were visible from the gaps of the collapsed wall, but there were no signs of life.

The area around the school swimming pool in the east section of First Middle School grounds was also a harrowing sight. Not just First Middle School teachers and students, but people with terrible burns, who had come from outside the school in search of water, had rushed to this place. Perhaps due to heat or dryness, many people, lost in a daze, had dived head first into the pool water and died like that or had got in the pool because they were unable to withstand the heat, but then lost strength and sunk into the water. Around the pool, many were lying down with bodies swollen to double their normal size due to the burns covering their entire bodies. Most were barely breathing, or had already breathed their last.

The first graders of the odd-numbered classes, who were working on the forced evacuation and demolition of buildings in the area behind City Hall, were experiencing the same wretchedness as the students at the school. They had been outside about one kilometer from ground zero. As they had been hit by the heat rays and bomb blast at the moment that Little Boy exploded, most of them suffered terrible burns and cuts to their entire body. Many died instantly, and many that still survived were mortally wounded.

Where the public hall's pond was, north of City Hall, many City Hall employees and bomb victims in the area had jumped into the pond trying to escape from the heat, but most of these people were already dying.

At the same time that Yoshio at First Middle School had been struck by the violent flash, Kiyosuke in Yokogawa-cho had arrived at his company, situated close to his home. In the office, Kiyosuke suddenly felt a flash like burning magnesium fill the entire room and he instinctively covered his body. Directly after, the fierce impact struck. When he came to, he was buried under the collapsed building. With a struggle, Kiyosuke managed to crawl out through a gap in the rubble. His left arm was bleeding from some minor cuts, but, fortunately, he had not suffered any terrible burns. Kiyosuke instinctively thought that his company had taken a direct hit but when he looked outside, most of the buildings around him had collapsed. Fires were already beginning to flare up. He hurriedly turned to return to the house, but flames were already rising from the flattened home, and there was nothing he could do about it. Looking toward Hiroshima's city center, he could see plumes of smoke rising up everywhere over there as well.

Kiyosuke couldn't comprehend at all what had happened. Looking at the plumes of smoke engulfing the entire city of Hiroshima, he thought of Seiji who was a military serviceman posted to the Military District Command Headquarters inside Hiroshima Castle, and of Yoshio who was at First Middle School. However, everywhere around him, flames were already beginning to flare up from various places among the collapsed houses, and it was not possible to head into the city center to make sure that Seiji and Yoshio were safe. As it was dangerous to stay there where he was, Kiyosuke decided to leave the burning town of Yokogawa-cho behind and flee to Midorii Village, which was an evacuation destination.

On the road heading out of town from Yokogawa-cho, there were already many victims lying on the road, as if they had fallen down unable to move any further. Many of them had suffered terrible burns. As he also was injured, Kiyosuke was unable to care for them, and with sorrowful feelings, he blended into the throng of evacuees that completely filled the road, and headed for Midorii Village.

Seiji, that day, was in the accounting department of Military District Headquarters in Hiroshima Castle. He had been transferred to the accounting department of the Military District Headquarters from the Manchukuo 815th Division in June of that year to serve as an apprentice officer. Seiji was happy he had been able to return to hometown Hiroshima. Motomachi (Motomachi, Naka Ward, Hiroshima), where the military district headquarters was located, was just a stone's throw away from Yokogawa-cho.

On the morning of that day, Seiji had been unable to get enough sleep because alerts were issued many times that past night. At 7:31 a.m. the alert was lifted, and finally heaving a sigh of relief, he together with other officer cadets went to the barracks and lay down to catch a bit of sleep.

After 8:00 a.m., Seiji heard a roar from high in the sky, but as no alert had been issued, he stayed where he was lying down. In the next moment, a flash filled the entire room, and directly after, the barracks collapsed. Although Seiji received minor injuries to his head and right arm, being inside the building saved him from getting burned, and he somehow managed to crawl out from the collapsed building. His colleagues with whom he had taken a nap together in the barracks had mostly been killed by being crushed by the collapsed building. A ceiling beam that had fallen had created a gap just were Seiji was lying down.

Having been rescued by this, Seiji soon found refuge at the Fukuya Department Store, which had only its exterior damaged by the explosion.

Hiroshi, that day, was on Etajima Island. After 8:00 a.m., a gigantic smoke plume, accompanied by a massive boom, rose up in the direction of the city of Hiroshima. Many of the houses on the north side of the island, which faces Hiroshima, had the glass of their windows break. Soon, the news was passed around the island residents that Hiroshima had suffered something terrible. The conversations mentioned that it must have been something like a large explosion at an explosives warehouse or a gas tank explosion, or something. Hiroshi looked at the scene of Hiroshima, which could be seen as a distant view from the island, and he instinctively knew that this was something very serious. Although he was worried for his father and brothers, the sea passage was in chaos with ships carrying victims to the minor islands, and it was impossible to immediately return from Etajima Island to Hiroshima. It took more than a day before Hiroshi was able to return to Hiroshima.

Hiroshi arrived at Ujina Port by ship from Etajima, and gulped. The pier was crowded with victims with appearances that made you want to look away. They were mostly like living ghosts. For a while he was unable to determine just what had happened at Hiroshima. Feeling confused, he decided at any rate to return to his home. With smoke still rising from here and there, Hiroshi desperately made his way along the roads covered in rubble until he finally came home to Yokogawa-cho. His home, however, was completely destroyed, and nothing at all remained. There was simply a notice board standing there stating in Kiyosuke's handwriting that he had fled to the evacuation place at Midorii Village. Not knowing of Seiji's or Yoshio's safety, Hiroshi hurried to Midorii Village. Upon arriving at the evacuation place at Midorii Village, Hiroshi was able to reunite with his father who was out of harm's way. However, neither Seiji nor Yoshio was there.

In the afternoon of August 6, the Clothing Depot at Deshio-cho was crowded with victims who had been carried from Hiroshima's city center. Inside the building, there was nowhere to put one's foot due the place being so crammed with the victims that had been brought in. Most of the people had been mortally injured and were suffering terrible burns and wounds. Inside, it was filled with moans and repeated cries for, "water, water . . ." These sounds echoed throughout the building.

Although it was a first-aid station for the victims, at best, the only aid that could be given to the burns was to apply merbromin solution or zinc oxide oil. Suffering from terrible thirst, most people ignored the rice ball placed on their pillow and solely cried out for water. However, the people charged with first-aid had been told that the victims would die if they were given water, and giving them water was prohibited. Even so, feeling so sorry for them, some of the first-aid workers secretly gave them water. Then, many of the people who received water drank with particular gusto and shortly died thereafter.

There was practically nothing that could be done to help Yoshio, who had been brought in to the Clothing Depot, as he had received burns to his entire body. Inside Yoshio's body, his heart was beating faintly, and his lungs were taking in barely any air. In a short while, Yoshio's vital organs stopped.

From Yoshio's name tag sewn to the breast area of his uniform, it was possible to determine his name, address and age. After writing these details along with his date of death down on the victims' register, his corpse was taken together with the continuously increasing mass of dead bodies and cremated at a nearby field.

The time that the news of the harrowing situation at Hiroshima first reached Tokyo on August 6 was at 8:30 a.m. Directly after Little Boy was dropped on Hiroshima, the Air Defense Command Post at the Naval Base at Kure observed a flash and a large explosion in the sky above Hiroshima, which was directly followed by a massive mushroom cloud spiraling upward. The Kure Naval Base telephoned the 2nd General

Military Headquarters in Hiroshima to get some detailed information, but there was no answer. As a result, they telephoned the Imperial Headquarters in Tokyo to report the calamity at Hiroshima. On receiving this information, Tokyo also attempted to contact Hiroshima but there was absolutely no line. Unable to find out any detailed circumstances, they first of all decided to dispatch an investigation team. In Tokyo, Imperial Headquarters, knowing that Hiroshima had suffered significant damage from a bomb dropped by a B-29, but still not having a proper grasp of the circumstances, made the following announcement to the people in the afternoon of August 7.

Announcement by Imperial Headquarters, 15:30, August 7, 1945

1. On August 6, Hiroshima received considerable damage from an attack by a few enemy B-29s.

2. It appears the enemy has used a new type of bomb in the attack, and investigations are ongoing.

Chapter 5 Reminiscence

Many of the people in Hiroshima who survived August 6, 1945, were left emotionally scarred by the fact that their close relatives and people dearest to them had suddenly vanished from this world.

Dropped from high in the sky above Hiroshima, Little Boy had exploded 600 meters above the ground some 250 meters south east of the aiming point, Aioi Bridge. Shima Hospital, which was directly beneath, and mostly everything within a radius of several hundred meters disintegrated in a split second due to the 10,000 degree Celsius heat rays and the bomb blast estimated at 440 meters per second. In the area of several hundred meters from the actual ground zero, human bodies disappeared instantaneously without leaving a trace due to the high temperature immediately following the atomic explosion.

Even further away from ground zero than that, there were countless people whose bodies were dispersed and incinerated by the violent bomb blast and heat rays. There were also countless people who suffered terrible burns that made them unrecognizable, which meant they died without any relatives by their side.

At the time Yoshio passed away at the Clothing Depot on August 7, Kiyosuke was frantically looking throughout Hiroshima to find out if Yoshio was safe. Hiroshi, who had been on Etajima, had returned safely to the evacuation point Midorii Village, and he knew that Seiji was being accommodated at the Fukuya Department Store and that his life was not in danger. However, he didn't have any news of Yoshio who should have gone to First Middle School.

As Yoshio had left his home to go to First Middle School to perform air defense personnel duties on the morning of August 6, it is believed he must have been struck by the bomb at the school. The next day, Kiyosuke, himself carrying minor injuries, headed for the city center of Hiroshima from Midorii Village. He passed Yokogawa-cho, and as he approached Hiroshima's city center, he couldn't believe the scene that filled his vision. Except for parts of buildings, Hiroshima's city streetscape had completely vanished. When he arrived in front of Aioi Bridge, he cast his eyes upon the circular dome that had been the key feature of the Industrial Promotion Hall located just south of the bridge. The circumference of the dome, located in the center of the building, was all that remained, and the larger half of the Industrial Promotion Hall had been destroyed.

When he turned his eyes to the Motoyasu River that runs alongside, innumerable corpses were floating there, completely covering the river surface. The corpses, all similarly strange and bloated, formed a single, lumped-together group, a bobbing mass completely disassociated with human bodies, which slowly moved with the flow of the river. Gazing at this sight, Kiyosuke thought it strange that while looking upon so many corpses, he was already numb to the horror.

Looking east across the Aioi Bridge with its railings blown away, apart from the bank and the life insurance company standing in Kamiya-cho (Kamiya-cho, Naka Ward, Hiroshima), the only other buildings left in that direction were the Fukuya Department Store and the Chugoku Newspaper Company located much further away. As a result, the small Mt. Hiji on the eastern side of the Kyobashi River, up until now hidden behind buildings, appeared as if it were right before one's eyes. Turning his gaze, he looked south to where First Middle School should have been. He could see the Hiroshima Branch of the Bank of Japan and Chugoku Electric Power Company. Further beyond that, Ninoshima Island and Etajima Island, floating on Hiroshima Bay, seemed so uncannily close. Then looking far away toward the west, it was even possible to see Miyajima Island. Apart from these scorched and blackened buildings that remained, the city of Hiroshima had changed into a spectacle of rubble strewn flat across the whole surface.

What on earth had happened? Kiyosuke had experienced the violent flash and impact when at his company's office on the morning of the sixth. During the moment, he thought he had been directly hit. Because the impact happened just once, Kiyosuke thought that just his own company had received a direct impact. And so after crawling out from under the collapsed building and seeing that not just Yokogawa-cho, but the entire city of Hiroshima was burning, Kiyosuke was unable to comprehend what on earth had happened. Now, having come to see Hiroshima's city center, Kiyosuke once again felt bewildered. There was nothing at all left of the city of Hiroshima.

The aftermath of destruction gradually became more terrible as he approached the center of the city. Smoke was still rising from here and there among the ruins. Along the road, fallen telegraph poles and power lines blocked the path, and the way forward was cut off many times. The asphalt paving was so hot that it felt as if it may burn the feet even walking with shoes. Scattered about everywhere were the charred corpses, still uncollected. A stench of death engulfed the entire city.

Along the tramway, a tram that had deviated from its course and derailed had been left completely burned. Kiyosuke noticed what looked

Scene of First Middle School after the bomb (the gate posts of the front gate remain)
Provided by H. J. Perterson – Hiroshima Peace Memorial Museum

like human figures inside the street car. He took a closer look at the vehicle, thinking there may be someone still alive, and gulped. The human figures were countless corpses standing rigid, still gripping the leather straps as if they had died instantly when struck by the heat rays. In many cases, their upper bodies were horribly burned, but from their waist down, nothing but bone remained. And lying on top of one another on the floor inside the car, the severely charred corpses were no longer recognizable as men or women.

Kiyosuke arrived at First Middle School in Zakoba-machi (Kokutaijimachi, Naka Ward, Hiroshima City) and stood frozen in amazement in front of the school gates. Inside the school grounds, like the other areas inside the city, nothing but rubble remained of not just the school building but everything else. Everything, that was, except for the stone granite columns standing left and right of the gate, and a stone monument standing on the right, when coming inside the gate, that was erected to commemorate a visit by His Imperial Highness the Crown Prince. These served as the only indication that this was once First Middle School. Other than that, nothing was left of the front main building, the lecture hall that should have been to its right, or the one-story wooden classrooms that had stood in a line behind the main building.

At the time Kiyosuke had gone to the school, smoke was still rising here and there from the burned-down school. Where the school building had been, aluminum lunch boxes and unburned bones lay strewn about. Over at the sports field on the south side of the school, numerous bodies, mostly First Middle School students, were lying on the ground. During this time, Kiyosuke had been walking around looking for Yoshio, but he couldn't find him. They were already dead and appearing like lumps of flesh, dark reddish and bloated from terrible burns. None of the corpses were recognizable just by looking at them, but the First Middle School students were painstakingly identified by the name tags sewn to the breast area of their uniforms.

When Kiyosuke returned inside the school grounds and went to the pool area in the eastern part of the grounds, it was all too horrible for the eyes there as well. Inside the pool, there were so many corpses that you couldn't see the surface of the water. Most of the bodies were entirely covered in burns, and as they were submerged in water, they were bloated to the point of no longer appearing human. Let alone age, even their sex was indiscernible. There were many First Middle School students, but Kiyosuke was unable to recognize Yoshio from among them.

In despair, Kiyosuke returned to the front gate. There, several teachers and upper-grade students who had escaped the bomb were waiting under a hut made from galvanized sheet metal. They were receiving inquiries from relatives concerning the safety of students. Kiyosuke inquired about Yoshio, but they were unable to help. However, as he heard that many of the students struck by the bomb at the school were carried to Ninoshima Island and Kanawajima Island, he also travelled to those two islands but he couldn't find any news of Yoshio. He also searched for Yoshio aimlessly at rescue centers in various regions, including the Red Cross Hospital at Senda-machi (Senda-machi, Naka Ward, Hiroshima City), but he could find no clues.

Finally Kiyosuke gave up trying to find news of Yoshio. Considering the harrowing scene at First Middle School, he came to believe that any of the skeletal remains inside the school could have been Yoshio. Moreover, even if he had been rescued, he thought there was next to no chance that Yoshio was still alive. He had to come to this conclusion. What else could he possibly have done? Amid such a situation where one city had been destroyed in an instant, one wonders how many people were able to find family whose whereabouts was unknown. Even if Kiyosuke had reunited with Yoshio at the Clothing Depot, Yoshio would have been close to death. It is also possible that by the time Kiyosuke went, Yoshio would have been dead and cremated. Remember, Yoshio's remains and all belongings that he had with him on that day were never returned to the family.

The history that followed the dropping of the atomic bomb on Hiroshima, a first in human history, is probably already known by most readers. Two days later on August 8, the Soviet Union abruptly unilaterally cancelled the Soviet-Japanese Neutrality Pact, declared war on Japan, and began an invasion into Manchukuo. On August 9, the second atomic bomb was dropped on Nagasaki. In response to this, the Japanese government accepted the Potsdam Declaration, and on August 15, Japan surrendered unconditionally to the Allied Powers.

The war was over. For Kiyosuke's family, it remained unknown what happened to Yoshio, but Seiji and Hiroshi had fortunately survived. The family, having lost their home in Yokogawa-cho, for the time being, continued their life at their place of evacuation in Midorii Village. Having been injured, Seiji was moved from the Fukuya Department store, which had taken him in, to the Hiroshima Red Cross Hospital where he spent some time hospitalized. Then on October 31, he left hospital and returned to the family at the evacuation place in Midorii Village. Although Kiyosuke and Seiji were bomb survivors, they fortunately did not suffer illness from the atomic bomb.

Kiyosuke's first challenge was to obtain a way to make a living. His company in Misasa-machi had unfortunately been turned into ashes, and he was forced to start again from scratch. Luckily, however, Kiyosuke's most trusted employee at the company, Mr. Hirayama had survived, and Kiyosuke was also able to get in contact with customers and trading partners who had also escaped harm. Although it happened a little bit at a time, while doing odd jobs, he managed to resurrect the company. Moreover, Seiji joined Chugoku Electric Power Company in July of 1946, and it became possible to support the family's living. Hiroshi was prone to illness, and so he continued a life of convalescence in the home at the evacuation place.

When the war ended, Japanese in the overseas territories were repatriated. Among the returnees were Seiji and Hiroshi's female cousin. The cousin had returned safely from the Korean Peninsula to her family home in Shimonoseki. After hearing of the atomic bomb dropping on Hiroshima and how Yoshio was victim to it, she sent the following letter to Seiji.

<Letter stamped January 23, 1946>
(Sender) Kazuko Morita, 46 Nagato-machi Shimonoseki
(Addressee) Seiji Kanaya, Hachishiki, Midorii Village, Asa District, Hiroshima Prefecture

Dear Seiji

The news of the cessation of war arrived on August 15, and feeling miserable about our defeat in the colonies, I swallowed my tears and returned from the Korean Peninsula. I came home to Japan to find my family home had burned down with nothing remaining.

On hearing of Hiroshima, the unspeakable cruelness pains my heart. There are simply no words of sympathies or condolences for such a thing. How has your body been healing since?

As for dear Yoshi, my thoughts are with your family during this trying time. I can still so vividly recall the image of dear Yoshi with all his vigor. I thought you may be wishing for a recent photo of Yoshi. I enclose a photo with this letter thinking it may be well received.

On a different note, I had been constantly thinking I should bring that law textbook that you left at my house. But it burned along with the house. I sincerely apologize. Please forgive me.

Please take good care of yourself in this cold weather.

With various condolences and apologies. . . Until I visit. . .

Kazuko

Although life as evacuees in Midorii Village proved arduous both physically and mentally, the three family members, Kiyosuke, Seiji and Hiroshi, somehow managed to continue to lead a day-to-day existence. However, illness-prone Hiroshi's physical condition gradually deteriorated, perhaps due to the poor dietary circumstances at the time. Then, in the middle of the night of April 27, 1947, with Kiyosuke and Seiji by his side, Hiroshi passed away. He died aged 25. Kiyosuke had lost his wife Futayo and his fourth son Yoshio in 1945, and now two years later, is second son. The family was now just himself and first born Seiji.

Even for one as brave as Kiyosuke, losing another son after Yoshio was naturally a huge devastation. Even so, he had to continue with the company in order to make a living. In August of that year, two years after the bomb was dropped, Kiyosuke went on a business trip to Otaru, Hokkaido, to buy fish for fertilizer raw material. The letter he wrote while on that trip gives a good insight into his feelings at that time.

<Letter stamped August 1, 1947>
(Sender) Kiyosuke Kanaya, Tokiyasu, Shinonome-cho, Otaru City
(Addressee) Seiji Kanaya, Hachishiki, Midorii Village, Asa District, Hiroshima Prefecture

Dear Seiji,
I arrived in Tokyo on the 23rd and then in Hakodate at 5 p.m. on the 28th, where I stayed because of damage in the Tohoku area and irregular scheduling of the steam train. I stayed there for two days on the 28 and 29th, and then I arrived at Otaru at 5 p.m. on the 30th.
Although it is outside the regulations for fish fertilizers, as ?? is 1/20th the 100 yen level it is attractive for its price, and even doing ????, it looks like it will be difficult to make it anything but a partial

ingredient. I think we have to rely on foods. As my trip was hurried, I did not bring a contract with an understanding of the foods ingredient circumstances. I'm finding it difficult to secure purchases. I will be here the 30th, 31st, and quite possibly stay as long as three days. As no other purchase opportunities are presenting themselves, it is a struggle. Under these circumstances, I won't be able to come home, as if someone came home now, one or two people would have to stay here for a long time. At any rate, the original plan of returning on the fourth or the fifth is no longer possible.

For the morning of the sixth (around 9:00), can you please on my behalf go to Otake and make immediate inquiries to Koryu temple, and ask the Furukawas and the Okinos etc. as part of preparations for the third anniversary of Yoshio's death. The sixth is also the date for Aunt Okino. While riding the steam train, and while sleeping at the inn, when I think of Hiroshi's death, these days I think more of how young Yoshio was, so full of energy and spirit. I can't help but think of all those good points. You're now my one and only, Seiji. You're the only purpose that I have in rebuilding the Kanaya household. And so for the many years ahead, I will principally think about you, and I wish to be as a guardian to you.

Sincerely,

Your Father.

August 1, (in Tokiyasu, Shinonome-cho Otaru City)

Meanwhile, at First Middle School, Yoshio's school, efforts had begun to rebuild the school. In December 1945, Takeo Kazuta was appointed the 15th school principal, and borrowing the military hospital building located in Eba (Eba-cho, Naka Ward, Hiroshima City), the school restarted classes in January of the following year.

Already in 1945, from among the students of Yoshio's year who had survived, the idea was put forward to meet on August 6 of the following year for the first memorial anniversary and create a compilation of memorial prose. One of the students playing a central role in this, along with the teachers, was Heitaro Hamada. The theme name for the prose was decided to be a "spring." The theme name "Spring" was taken from "Old nostalgic memories well up like a spring," which was part of a prose written by Hiroyuki Doida, who was on air-defense personnel duty at the school on the day of the bomb and had lived through it. Based on a proposal by Hamada, it was decided to draw spiderwort on the cover. Much spiderwort had been growing around the front yard and greenhouse of the biology classroom, and purple was the color of the First Middle School flag.

This collection of prose was published by Hiroshima Kosan Company, Limited. This company was Hiroshima Aviation before the war, and First Middle School students had worked there as part of labor mobilization. Thanks to this connection, Hamada visited the company's president Soichi Taguchi and asked if they would publish the compilation, and he agreed to publish it.

In this "Spring" Volume 1, a student in the same year wrote about Yoshio. His name was Tadayuki Abe.

"Thoughts of Yoshio, my departed friend" Tadayuki Abe, Grade 4

After meeting each other at the beginning of second year, Yoshio and I studied together and played together. Now it still seems just a dream that he has gone.

Yoshio and I were close through model airplane making. Before mobilization, we often met to talk about airplanes. He was an expert on airplanes, and whenever I asked him about something, there was never a time when he did not know, and he patiently explained it to me. On holidays, we would take the gliders and airplanes we made and join many other friends at the Eastern Parade Ground to try flying them. There were times when we had fun for the whole day. Also even today, I can remember vividly the gliding training.

I think everyone was familiar with him wearing a white flying cap he made himself, doing his operation by giving his own original, slightly excited orders, and the way he used to run up to the teacher.

Even while we were at mobilization, during our small breaks, we would talk about the American and British planes. There truly wasn't anyone else who knew more about American, British and Japanese aircraft.

If he were still alive today, I'm sure that in addition to grieving, he would definitely rise to the occasion and put in all his efforts for a new Japan.

We will carry on his spirit while working for a new Japan. We must strive to do his share, two people's share or three people's share for the nation.

I would like to think he would look from beneath the shadows of the grass with joy and relief if we stuck to these plans.

"Spring" Volume 1, published August 1, 1946. Published by Hiroshima Kosan Company, Limited.

I knew that Mr. Abe was close to Yoshio, and although I felt rude to do so, I wrote to Mr. Abe asking for him to tell me what he knew about Yoshio. After a short while, he sent the following reply.

Dear Mr. Kanaya,

Thank you for giving me the opportunity to read the precious materials the other day. I became immersed in my memories as a junior-high second grader so long ago.

Although Yoshio was tall, he was put in the front of the classroom (perhaps because he wore glasses). As a result, he became a friend in my group.

At the time, there were gliding drills on the Eastern Parade Ground where we could ride gliders. The glider was launched into the air by stretching out a rubber rope in a V-shape. At best we rode once or twice in one day, and pulled the rubber rope. Over several times, we got better at it. I managed to fly 20 or 30 centimeters above the ground. I still haven't forgotten the thrill of lifting up into the sky.

Yoshio was good at it. I think he managed 1 to 1.5 meters. His unique style and behavior are still etched in my memory. This led to our enthusiasm for creating airplanes and gliders. We weren't satisfied with existing products. We also created gliders from our own new designs and made various modifications as we went.

I have a memory of when we were at Toyo Kogyo. At the time it was manufacturing 38 type infantry rifles rather than cars. About 150 of us were given the job of disassembling the rifles and polishing the parts. A day's work was extremely painstaking. For example, while waiting for the steam train at Hiroshima Station or Mukainada Station, we had to stand silently in line. Lunch time at the factory was likewise spent in silence as well.

During the forced building evacuation work, 150 of us were divided into two teams. We took turns working around Tsurumibashi. I don't have any memory of Dobashi. Therefore, I think that the fact that he died on August 7 means he most likely was hit by the bomb at First Middle School while performing air defense personnel duties.

I searched to see if I had some memorabilia. But as my house at 1-chome, Minami-machi, was bombed and I evacuated to Ono Town where I am now, there was none. It's a pity. It is now a long time ago, but I am deeply grateful for the opportunity to reminisce about Yoshio. I think that he is looking down from heaven, pleased to see his nephew Toshinori collecting these materials.

I wish you successful endeavors.

Yours sincerely,

Tadayuki Abe

May 8, 2008.

In Mr. Abe's letter, he wrote that it was most likely that Yoshio was performing air defense personnel duties when the bomb hit. When I read this, it was both startling and useful knowledge for me. Actually, at that time, I did not know Yoshio had gone to First Middle School to perform air defense personnel duties. Rather, I thought he had been hit by the bomb around either Dobashi or Tsurumibashi, while working on labor mobilization like the other third graders.

As luck would have it, at the time that I received a letter from Mr. Abe, I had the opportunity to get my hands on "My Hiroshima Map" written by the author Shiro Nakayama. Mr. Nakayama was also a third grader at First Middle School in the same year as Yoshio when the bomb hit. He has produced several works that were themed on this experience. When I read "My Hiroshima Map," it had mentioned the air defense personnel but at the time, I hadn't even considered that Yoshio had been serving as air defense personnel on that day. Therefore, my interest was focused on Mr. Nakayama and the other third graders who were close to Tsurumibashi when the bomb hit.

It is known that that locations of the third graders of First Middle School on August 6 when the bomb dropped were Toyo Kogyo (Fuchu Town, Aki District), Kansai Kosakujo (Funairi-Kawaguchi-cho, Naka Ward, Hiroshima), Dobashi area (Sakai-machi, Naka Ward, Hiroshima) and in the Tsurumibashi area (from Higashihiratsuka-cho to Tsurumi-cho, Naka Ward, Hiroshima City). All locations were for either labor mobilization or mobilization for the forced building evacuation and demolition. Among them, Toyo Kogyo and Kansai Kosakujo were far from ground zero, and very few students died there. As Dobashi and Tsurumibashi were close to ground zero and the forced building evacuation and demolition work was outside, the injuries were great. This was particularly so for the students hit by the bomb around Dobashi. At some eight hundred meters from ground zero, they all died. However, as Sakai-machi of the Dobashi vicinity is west from ground zero, if Yoshio had been hit by the bomb at Dobashi, he would have been taken to a facility located west of Hiroshima's city center. On the other hand, the Tsurumibashi vicinity is east from ground zero. Considering that the Clothing Depot where Yoshio was taken was a facility on the east side, I had concluded that Yoshio had been one of the third graders mobilized close to Tsurumibashi when the bomb struck.

I thought that Mr Nakayama, who had been hit by the bomb close to Tsurumibashi, may have been together with Yoshio and have some new information. With this hope in mind, I sent him a letter. In a short while, Mr. Nakayama replied and contrary to my expectations, my assumptions were off the mark. According to Mr. Nakayama's letter, although all the third graders mobilized to the Tsurumibashi area were burned by the blast, there were not any students who died immediately after, probably because they were 1.5 kilometers from ground zero. Mr. Nakayama also informed me that Yoshio was most probably serving as air defense personnel at First Middle School when the bomb exploded.

It was these letters from Mr. Abe and Mr. Nakayama that led me to believe that Yoshio could only have been performing air defense personnel duties at First Middle School. I heard that one of the third graders who was serving as air defense personnel, had survived the bomb and was still alive. His name was Hiroyuki Doida. In "Yukari no Tomo" published by the Hiroshima Prefectural Hiroshima First Middle School Bomb Survivor Students Association, there was a contribution by Hidetsugu Nakajima, a teacher at First Middle School at the time who escaped the bomb blast by being in the First Middle School Dormitory in Midori

Machi (Midori-machi, Hiroshima City). He wrote that the dozen or so third graders on air defense personnel duty, except one student who was miraculously saved while working since the previous night (Masayuki Doida), all perished. The real name was "Hiroyuki Doida" not "Masayuki Doida." Mr. Nakajima had either remembered incorrectly or it had been a printing error. Only the name "Hiroyuki Doida" is listed in the alumni directory, so it was definitely the same person.

After graduating from First Middle School, Mr. Doida went on to Keio University and afterwards joined the Bank of Tokyo. In 1950, he was selected by the Japanese soccer team to play in the Asia Cup. After that, he was an advisor for Shimizu S-Pulse. The Second Volume of "Spring," writes about Mr. Doida on the morning of August 6. Having finished his duties as air defense personnel, he was walking down the school corridor holding an empty bucket. He heard a roaring sound and so he put the bucket over his head and looked at the B-29 in the sky. It was then that the bomb hit. When he came too, he was buried under the corridor with the bucket covering his head. He apparently then crossed Miyukibashi Bridge, and escaped to the same first-aid post, the Clothing Depot, that Yoshio had been taken to. As I thought that perhaps he may know something about what happened to Yoshio at that time, I sent Mr. Doida a letter, in high hopes. However, the letter that arrived not long after was from his wife. Mr. Doida had unfortunately already passed away in 1995. Incidentally, I later learned that according to "Spring" Volume II, Mr. Doida had worked on the compilation of "Spring" Volume I with Mr. Hamada.

Following this, I continued to send letters to several still-surviving men who were in the same year as Yoshio. Among this correspondence, I exchanged letters several times with Mr. Hamada and Mr. Susumu Zoriki. This correspondence provided quite a bit of information on Yoshio at that time.

Mr. Hamada, was multi-talented and active in mountain climbing, photography, avant-garde calligraphy, and essay writing. Two years prior, he had a hand in publishing "Spring" Volume II. Mr. Zoriki organized the "Hiroshima First Middle School 1948 Reunion" (a reunion for 1948 graduates of Hiroshima First Middle School). As he was someone with detailed knowledge concerning information on his fellow classmates, and an incredibly sharp memory, I asked him to ask fellow classmates about any information concerning Yoshio, and he told me a lot of detailed information about that time.

Both men apparently were in different classes from Yoshio. However, according to a letter from Mr. Zoriki, his memory of Yoshio was as follows: "My relationship with Yoshio Kanaya was not that close because our houses were not close and we were in different classes. But he wore glasses, was fair complexioned, was gentle natured and had a sturdy body. He talked to me like a kindly older brother. His gentle nature still remains strongly etched in my memory. Even now I can picture him in front of me as a Hiroshima First Middle School student with gaiters rolled and wearing a field cap."

When Yoshio was a third grader, his class was Class 31. Based on the information from various people, as the third graders were spending all day every day performing labor mobilization duties in 1945, the students of the same class rarely saw each other in the classroom. Partly due to this, I could not find anyone who was close to Yoshio apart from Mr. Abe.

Then, on one of the days I was searching for information on Yoshio, I received a letter from Mr. Nakayama that contained a copy of the following article written by him in a newspaper column.

"It's once again the loquat season in the greengrocers.

Every year, when I see those egg-shaped fruit that ripen to a yellowish orange, I remember the day I went picking loquat at this time of year in 1945.

At the time, I was a third grader at a junior high school in Hiroshima.

In accordance with the Student Mobilization Order, we had been mobilized since the second term of second grade, and we were working in a factory.

The food we received from the factory was a staple diet of soybean and sorghum with grasshopper boiled in soy and two or three slices of pickled daikon radish. It was very lacking in nourishment, and the servings were measly. Being growing children, and having to carry out weapons production work standing in front of machinery for two shifts, the mobilized students were always feeling hungry.

One day, when the teacher announced that we would use the day off from the factory to go picking loquats, our hearts lifted and waited for that day with great eagerness. We went to a place that we call the loquat mountain, located in a town called Furue in the western outskirts of the city close to the Seto Inland Sea. No one had harvested the fruit and the trees were laden with ripe fruit, we freely ate the sweet plump ripe fruit to our heart's content.

Not long afterward, the bomb was dropped on Hiroshima and 60 students from our year were suddenly taken from this earth.

Thinking back on that day now, the loquat picking was perhaps our farewell ceremony."

While reading this, I was unable to stem the tears. The day of loquat picking written about by Mr. Nakayama was coincidentally also mentioned in one of Yoshio's letters. While I was reading, it was as if Mr. Nakayama's piece was overlapping with a section of letter right before my eyes. (See page XX.) When he wrote that carefree letter, Yoshio had no idea that his life would be suddenly taken from him not long after. My heart felt like it had been stabbed. I realized anew that this same Yoshio had in fact died in the explosion of the atom bomb.

I continued to get in contact with the people who were in the same school year as Yoshio. In addition to the people who were introduced by

Mr. Hamada and Mr. Zoriki, I also was introduced to people who were third graders at the time of the bomb from articles related to the bomb in newspapers. When I sent letters to these people, I received a reply from one person, a Mr. Yoshio Kato.

Mr. Kato had wished to join the junior air cadets after entering Hiroshima First Middle School. He apparently spent from dawn to dusk glider practicing on the Eastern Parade Grounds while a student. After the war, he turned to Christianity and had devoted himself to community service. In response to the letter he received from me, Mr. Kato sent the following reply.

Dear Mr. Kanaya

This year's summer is particularly hot. I expect we are mutually struggling with the heat.

Reading about Yoshio Kanaya at the time of the bomb, there were some names that brought back fond memories, names that I remember, and names that I forgot. I feel it would be rude to say I don't know any of the names.

But I am sure that all the alumni would remember the name Yoshio Kanaya. He commuted to school from Yokogawa-cho north of Hiroshima's city center. He was famous within the school.

I was commuting from a country town in Gion Village in Asa District (Gion, Asaminami Ward, Hiroshima). I would ride the Kabe line from there to Yokogawa, where we would form lines according to school and walk in formation to school. Yoshio was in the city group, the Yokogawa-cho and Misasa-machi group. They were the preppy group. The train commuters (Kabe line) were the hillbilly group (from the rural districts). And in those two groups, we would walk to school. It wasn't really like that. We walked to school in file in a two-row formation. We were proud of being students of Hiroshima First Middle School.

Yoshio was a handsome boy, city savvy and particularly popular with the female students. I mostly remember his ability to put on an air of perfect innocence, and more than anything else how particularly popular he was with the female students. Also, he was very popular among the city kids and the commuters from the country for his ability to talk on various things concerning airplanes, gliders, battleships and so on.

He was particularly knowledgeable about gliders and airplanes. He was kind to people and he even looked out for us country folk.

I remember working together at Mazda. However, they had introduced shifts (at the time of the A-bomb) and work switched between working at Mazda and working for the forced evacuation and demolition, and I don't know which now. On August 6, I'm not sure which was what. On that day, I was on forced evacuation and demolition work and we had assembled at Tsurumi-bashi. (My left upper body was burned.)

The booklet I have enclosed with the letter is a book that social services made for me when I reached retirement age for probation officer and welfare commissioner. I thought he was in a picture of a glider contained in the book. But it was a different glider. I am fifth from the left on the back row.

<Letter stamped September 1, 2010.>

From Mr. Kato's letter, like the letters of Mr. Abe and Mr. Zoriki, I was able to find out such things as his looks, personality, and an insight into daily life at school. The common element in all these people's tales is that Yoshio was clearly far more knowledgeable about aircraft than anyone else. Moreover the impression Yoshio's fellow students had of him was unexpectedly that of a mild mannered and quiet person. From these letters I learned that Yoshio was at First Middle School when the bomb hit, and I gained a vivid picture of Yoshio during his junior high school years. Incidentally, Mr. Kato passed away just two years after sending me that letter. I reverently express my condolences.

In this way, up until the present, people who were in the same year as Yoshio at First Middle School have been providing me with much precious information. Through my correspondence with people who had been in the same grade as Yoshio, I was struck by how willingly, thoroughly and politely every one of these people responded to me, a stranger.

While it helped that the high school I graduated from was the successor of Hiroshima First Middle School and that I belonged to the same alumni association, I think the larger reason for the tremendous response was their noble character. While they are now over eighty, I look up to them reverently. I admire and deeply respect their personalities and intelligence. When I think of Yoshio and how he spent his school life with these excellent fellow students, I think the second part of his life was not necessarily an unhappy time.

Notes

Epilogue

The people of Hiroshima refer to the atomic bomb as *pikadon* or just simply *pika*. These words are onomatopoeic in origin. At the moment the atomic bomb exploded, many people experienced a strong flash and bomb blast. Directly after the *pika* (flash), there was the *don* (boom). When I was a child, I often heard the words *pikadon* and *pika* spoken in the conversations of my family and various people.

In the mere several seconds that this *pikadon* lasted on August 6, 1945, many tens of thousands of people living in Hiroshima suddenly lost their lives. Most of the ten thousand or so people who died within a few hundred meters of ground zero were disintegrated by the intense heat, leaving no trace of body behind. Even as far away as one kilometer, many people's bodies were scattered and got burned up. And then there were an uncountable number of people, like Yoshio, who despite struggling to stay alive, ended up dying without any close relative by their side in their final moments.

Many of these people died without even realizing what had happened. It is possible that Yoshio also did not have the time to think back at what had happened to his body. Soldiers on the battlefield may have lost their lives in battle. And they may have met with circumstances to prepare for death. However the lives that were taken by pikadon were not those of soldiers on the battle field. They were mostly civilians, young and old, male and female, who were carrying out their daily lives in Hiroshima.

The death toll caused by the atomic bomb is actually not accurately known. There were no resources by which to verify the population of Hiroshima at the time. According to the result of a survey conducted by Hiroshima City in 1946 after the war, on the day of August 6, 1945, about 350,000 people in total were living in the city of Hiroshima, comprising about 312,000 civilians and 35,000 military personnel. In addition to this number, there were also people who had commuted from outside the city to companies and government offices, as well as people who had come to

Hiroshima for the forced evacuation and demolition work. Therefore, the number of people in Hiroshima when the atomic bomb was dropped is estimated to be between 370,000 and 400,000 people. The number of people who died within three months of the bomb dropping is said to be between 110,000 and 130,000 people. If we assume the number of people in the city at the time was 370,000 to 400,000, then that calculates to one in three people who died. Of course, the number of people who died later due to the aftereffects of injury was considerable. Based on these numbers, we know that so many people's lives were taken by this single atomic bomb.

Today, about seventy years after the dropping of the atomic bomb, the population of Hiroshima is over 570,000, even when only including the area inside the city boundaries that existed back then. It has recovered to become the core city in the Chugoku region. The people who visit Hiroshima for the first time probably have the impression that Hiroshima is no different from any other city apart from the memorial tourist sites such as the Atomic Dome and the Peace Museum. A few buildings from that time still remain. These are the so-called A-bombed buildings, left as legacies in various places in the city. However, looking at most of them from the outside, it is not possible to tell this.

On the other hand, there are more remnants of the horror that the city suffered from the atomic bomb than these tourist destinations and bombed buildings. These remnants can be seen in unexpected places. They can be seen if you visit the temple cemeteries throughout the city and look at the date of death inscribed on each tombstone. Among the tombstones, there are some that have had their corners blown away by the bomb blast, and some that have changed color due to heat-ray exposure. Then, separate to these tombstones, you will notice that among the tombstones erected after the war, there are many with the inscribed date of death of August 6, 1945, or on a date within several months of that date. Among those tombstones, there are many cases where one tombstone has the names of several people inscribed on it with the date of death of August 6, 1945. These are cases of families that lost almost all their family members to the atomic bomb. When one looks at tombstones of the deceased who died in childhood at that time, their lives were most likely taken by the bomb. It pains my heart to imagine the last moments for these children. Such places, unknown by tourists, quietly convey the fact that an atomic bomb was dropped on Hiroshima.

Now in the center of Hiroshima are streetscapes of modern buildings. Many of the people moving about in the city are going about their work, shopping, or dining as if nothing happened. This certainly may well be an indication of peace. If the bomb had not been dropped on Hiroshima some seventy years ago, the city would most likely have suffered heavy air raids like the other cities. Then it would never had become a city known throughout the world as a symbol of the horror of the atomic bomb, and it would now just be another ordinary regional city.

As I was born after the war, I, of course, never saw the horrible conditions caused by the atomic bomb. However, I have a renewed realization that an atomic bomb was dropped on this city. When I walk through the city, I always feel a suffering of some kind. This is because I sense that I can hear the wails and screams of the vast numbers of victims from beneath this city's ground, which is nowadays attractively paved with stone. I get overcome by the illusion that our feet treading on the paving are walking over the burnt bodies of the victims. It is likely that any person who experienced the atomic bomb feels more or less the same sensation in this city. Or perhaps this is an unusual sensation of mine formed by having grown up as a second-generation bomb victim.

Certainly, the atomic bomb brought about the most unimaginable tragedy to humans in all of human history. Apart from those people close to ground zero who died instantly when their bodies were annihilated by the explosion, the most common causes of death of those people who died within the few months after the atomic bomb dropped is thought to

146

have been due to serious burns and external injuries or due to acute radiation syndrome where massive radiation exposure caused extensive damage to bone marrow, digestive organs, or the central nervous system. Moreover, the atomic bomb was more than just a weapon that caused the mass destruction of vast numbers of people and buildings in an instant. The radioactive material that was dispersed by the nuclear fission caused frightening changes to cells in living bodies. Even if a patient recovered from the symptoms of the acute stage, they had health problems caused by various types of damage that lasted decades or an entire lifetime. If you are aware that people exposed to radiation such as from one of the nuclear power plant accidents that have occurred in various places in the world will continue to suffer aftereffects for many years after, and that the dispersion of radioactive material can have a huge impact on surrounding regions, then you can easily accept the fact that damage caused to a human body through radiation, such as what happened at Hiroshima, continues over a long period of time.

Certainly, if you describe the atomic bomb as one weapon used in war, then that is probably true enough. In the modern wars, particularly since the First World War, the shape of war has unmistakably changed through the development of weapons that had not been considered in earlier times such as bombers and poison gas. War up until then was a battle of only soldiers. From the First World War onward, war became an all-out war that used various weapons. It also resulted in many casualties as it entwined even people with no interest in war, including civilians. In the Second World War as well, both the Allied Powers and the Axis Powers openly conducted indiscriminate bombing and incendiary bombing of cities. Among these weapons, however, the atomic bomb has special characteristics that make it different from any other weapon. It disperses radioactive material that is extremely toxic to people over a wide area and it kills people indiscriminately.

Meanwhile, the atomic bomb was something never before seen in the history of mankind. The debate as to whether it was right or wrong to have dropped the atomic bomb began directly after bombs were dropped on Hiroshima and Nagasaki, and it has continued endlessly until now. The negative and affirmative propositions have become interwoven in the campaign for nuclear disarmament and the nuclear deterrent theory. Still now, it has not been possible to reach a conclusion upon which everyone can agree. I have neither the knowledge nor the ability to draw a conclusion on the rightfulness or wrongfulness of dropping the bomb. However, I can provide below some of the various opinions among people in the United States and elsewhere that have been expressed up until now concerning the rightfulness or wrongfulness of dropping the bomb.

Firstly, the United States formulated its reasons for dropping the bomb based on several background circumstances such as the following.

Firstly, in July 1945, when the Battle of Okinawa was nearing conclusion, the U.S. Military was planning its next operations against Japan. These were a landing operation of southern Kyushu on November 1, 1945, and a landing operation of Tokyo and its outskirts on March 1, 1946. The landing operation of the Japanese main islands, called Operation Downfall, was going to be the largest military operation in history. However, in the middle of the Potsdam Conference in July 1945, President Truman, knowing the nuclear testing was successful, stopped these operations, and it was agreed to conduct atomic bombing on Japan. The loss of US military lives in the Battle of Okinawa was higher than expected. On top of this, Truman was concerned over reports he received that as many as a million U.S. military lives could be lost if the military engagements with the Japanese military were similar to what was experienced in Okinawa. Truman supposed that if an atomic bomb were dropped, then Japan would probably quickly surrender and no landing operations on the Japanese main islands would be necessary. Thinking from a strategic perspective, it is natural that such a conclusion was reached.

Second, it was clearly evident that in the post-war international sphere expected to follow Japan's surrender, U.S.–Soviet friction would develop between the capitalist United States and the communist Soviet Union. Dropping the atomic bomb was considered to be a way of not only showing off U.S. military strength to the Soviet Union, but also preventing the Soviet Union from invading the Japanese main islands before Japan surrendered. For the United States, there was the policy-based reason that it would be beneficial for post-war Japan to be a capitalist nation like the United States so that Japan may serve as a seawall on the Pacific Ocean and cooperate with the United States in resisting the communist Soviet Union. In other words, there also were political motivations for using the atomic bomb.

The following historical background can be put forward as the basis for this. In July 1945, the Japanese government realized that it would lose the war. A special diplomatic plan was telegraphed to Japan's Ambassador to the Soviet Union for peace moves with the Soviet Union as mediator. This telegram was deciphered by the United States and relayed to President Truman, who was in Germany for the Potsdam Conference. Truman had entered into a secret pact with the Soviet Union for the Soviet Union to enter the war against Japan. At the same time, he had received reports concerning the success of nuclear testing and decided that the Soviet Union's participation in the war was unnecessary. Accordingly, he ignored the peace moves on the Japanese side and agreed to drop the atomic bomb. He also thought that by playing the atomic bomb as the trump card, he could achieve a stronger position against the Soviet Union. Certainly, if the atomic bomb had not been dropped, and if the Soviet Union had participated in the war against Japan, it could have resulted in Japan being split between the United States and the Soviet Union like what happened to post-war Germany. Therefore, under these second circumstances, it is natural that such a conclusion was reached from the perspective of using the atomic bomb as a trump card against the Soviet Union.

Third, as United States had invested a massive budget to develop the atomic bomb, it was in its interests to drop the atomic bomb to scientifically investigate the power of this weapon. Such investigation would include human experimentation. Moreover, the humans targeted for human experimentation were not white people of the same race as Americans. If the target country was Germany, one wonders whether the United States would have gone ahead and executed the atomic bombing. In other words there are people who assert that the bombing was against a backdrop of racial discrimination. On the basis of performing human experimentation, the Interim Committee chose medium-sized cities surrounded by mountains for most of the target candidate cities selected. Moreover, it forbid regular air raids on these target candidate cities and issued an absolute command to drop the atomic bomb by visual bombing so that the explosion would occur as close as possible to the aiming point. By 1945, most cities in Japan, including regional cities, had been turned into scorched earth by air raids. Yet a handful of large cities, including Hiroshima and Nagasaki, did not have any large air raids before the atomic bombing, which further supports the idea. Furthermore, not long after the war in 1948, the United States established the Atomic Bomb Casualty Commission to conduct biological and pathological research on the atomic bomb's impact on humans. The facility did not provide any medical treatment or assistance to the many bomb victims who were suffering before their eyes.

The opinion that the dropping of the atomic bomb on Japan was human experimentation is naturally not accepted by the United States. However, a judge representing India on the International Military Tribunal for the Far East, Radhabinod Pal stated the following.

"Famous philosopher of history Professor Toynbee expresses the following opinion: "When Westerners call a person of color or an Oriental a "native," the content of this word "native" excludes individual human rights and personality. It is simply a "moving tree" and an "animal that talks." Subliminally, this concept is boasting white supremacy with a consciousness of being "God's chosen people." According to Toynbee in other words, we Asians do not belong in the category of humans. That is why the atomic bomb was dropped on Hiroshima and Nagasaki: for the reason of animal experimentation. Probably in the Third World War, it will be on Asia where the hydrogen bombs and atomic bombs will be dropped. Certainly, it won't be on the white man." (Radhabinod Pal and Masaaki Tanaka. Judge Pal's 'Peace Declaration' Shogakukan)

I don't think anything stated above by Pal applies to today's international society. But even today, it is an undeniable truth that disputes and incidents based on racial discrimination are repeatedly surfacing in various locations around the world.

Furthermore, there are people with analytical opinions related to the personality of President Truman that assert the following. As a result of President Roosevelt's sudden death, Vice-President Truman was unexpectedly appointed as President. Truman who first knew of the Manhattan Project when he became president may have been in a position where he could not but approve the dropping of the atomic bomb as it had been developed over several years and funded by a massive nationally funded budget. Moreover, compared with President Roosevelt, who exhibited an emperor-like presence in the eyes of the American public, Truman was taunted as a failed haberdasher who had no backbone since childhood, and who never went to university. Therefore when he became president, he consciously reacted to disprove this image by following policies that externally appeared strong, and approving the dropping of the atomic bomb was strongly linked to this aspect of Truman's personality.

Even after the war, President Truman was consistent in continually asserting the validity of dropping the atomic bomb. The question of how much power Truman really had in issuing the command to conduct the atomic bombing is still a mystery. But it is clear that he did not appear to hold any remorse that the atomic bomb was dropped.

There was an anecdote told by the Secretary of State Dean Acheson. Several months after the atomic bomb had been dropped, Oppenheimer, who was in discussion with President Truman, commented that he had blood on his hands by developing the atomic bomb. Truman responded sarcastically suggesting that perhaps he should wipe off that blood. Then, after Oppenheimer departed, Truman stated that he never wanted to see that son of a bitch again.

Truman's motto was apparently "The buck stops here." If that were the case, then one can wonder how much responsibility that Truman felt for approving the dropping of the atomic bomb on Japan.

Of the above reasons, the first reason is the official view of the U.S. government. This reasoning forms the most convincing basis of the views of the people in the United States who believe the dropping of the atomic bomb was justified. These people consistently assert the argument that dropping the atomic bomb saved many young Americans from dying in the war. Moreover, it led to Japan surrendering earlier, and peace was achieved. It also prevented an invasion by the Soviet Union, and Japan was reborn as a democratic state. These reasons are given as justification for the dropping of the atomic bomb. People giving these reasons don't forget to add that if Japan had surrendered earlier, then it would not have been necessary to drop the bomb. Certainly, it is probably indisputable that Japan surrendered earlier as a result of the atomic bomb being dropped on Japan. It is also true that there were no dead and wounded from the U.S. military staging landing operation on Japan's main islands. Just hearing this, one would be of the opinion that the dropping of the atomic bomb is something to be thankful for, not just for the United States but for Japan as well. However, as I will now explain, the top echelons of the U.S. military were expecting Japan's surrender within the next several months regardless of whether or not the bomb was dropped.

Moreover, there was a possibility for surrender before the U.S. military staged a landing operation on Japan's main islands. Having lost control of the sea and control of the air, and with all citizens impoverished, Japan had no leeway to retaliate. Even if the U.S. military did not play its hand, I think it is glaringly obvious that Japan's surrender was imminent.

Alternatively, if the United States responded positively to the peace moves made by Japan, it would have been possible for Japan to make an early surrender, and it may have prevented the Soviet Union's participation in the war. The opinion asserting that a reduction in U.S. military casualties was achieved by dropping the atomic bomb could be seen as akin to accepting the argument that it is appropriate to inhumanely steal the lives of the enemy by whatever kind of means for the sake of reducing the sacrifice of one's own side. I believe that this foreign policy of the United States, which is consistently based on self-affirmation, is a characteristic of the United States' position in the Korean War, Vietnam War Iraq War and Afghanistan Conflict.

Responding to this rationale of justifying the dropping of the atomic bomb, there are also many people, particularly in the United States, who were against the dropping of the atomic bomb.

First, ironically, the people leading the opposition to the dropping of the nuclear bomb were the very scientists who advocated the theory of nuclear power and developed the nuclear bomb. Niels Bohr, who received the Nobel Prize for Physics for his research into atomic structure, the theoretical basis of atomic bomb development, was alarmed that the United States and Britain were developing nuclear power as a nuclear weapon. In order to urge the importance of controlling nuclear power through international pacts, he had already met with Prime Minister Churchill and President Roosevelt in 1944. However both these discussions had ended in disagreement.

Leo Szilard, who had promoted the development of nuclear weapons to President Roosevelt, collected together the signatures of 69 other scientists and submitted a letter in opposition to dropping the atomic bomb to President Truman on July 17, directly before the atomic bomb was dropped. However this letter was never read by Truman as he was at Potsdam when the letter was submitted. When the Interim Committee decided to drop an atomic bomb on Japan, seven scientists who participated in the Manhattan Project led by James Franck of the University of Chicago were against the dropping of the atomic bomb and submitted the "Franck Report" to Secretary of War Henry Stimson. This report also urged the control of nuclear weapons by an international pact and argued that if an atomic bomb were dropped on Japan, it would lead to an unstoppable nuclear arms race. The report, however, was not adopted.

The assertion shared by the scientists opposed to the dropping of the atomic bomb was that if an atomic bomb were dropped, the inhumane act of using this weapon would not only be censured by the world, but it would also inevitably lead to a nuclear arms race among various countries. Accordingly, they asserted it was necessary to prevent nuclear war by signing an international pact before this occurred. Then, as it happened, the history of mankind followed the very course they had warned against. Currently, as everyone is aware, nuclear arms are being developed in various countries, the number of countries that have nuclear weapons is increasing, and nuclear testing is continuing.

Second, and also ironically, there were many arguments against the dropping of the atomic bomb among U.S. military personnel. General Marshall, the U.S. Army Chief of Staff, had accepted the dropping of the atomic bomb. However, he asserted that the target candidates should be limited to military facilities and not cities, and that it should serve as a warning to Japan. He also held the view that Japan would probably surrender if it were on condition that the imperial system was preserved. General Eisenhower, Supreme Allied Commander in Europe, tried to convince Secretary of War Stimson that it was not desirable to drop the atomic bomb and be subject to the ire of world opinion because surrender was expected as Japan had already started looking for conditions for surrender and surrender was not far off. General MacArthur, Supreme Allied Commander in South West Pacific Area, believed, like Eisenhower, that Japan was already close to surrender. Yet he did not know of the plan to drop the atomic bomb until directly before. When he heard the report that an atomic bomb had been dropped on Hiroshima, he was reportedly furious. Admiral Leahy, Chief of Staff to the Commander in Chief, believed that neither the atomic bomb nor the landing operation on Japan's main islands would be required because Japan would surrender beforehand. Admiral Leahy also held the opinion that Japan would immediately surrender if it was a conditional surrender that preserved the imperial system. General Spaatz, commander of the U.S. Strategic Air Forces, who had signed the order to drop the atomic bomb also felt doubts about dropping the atomic bomb.

Third, among the politicians close to the president, Secretary of War Henry Stimson held doubts about dropping the atomic bomb after the war. When Kyoto was selected as one of the target candidate cities for the atomic bombing, Stimson was the person who was in strong opposition to this because the Japanese would never forgive the use of an atomic bomb on the old historical Kyoto for cultural and sentimental reasons. Moreover, Stimson had proposed a conditional surrender that included the preservation of the imperial system, but this proposal was rejected by President Truman and Secretary of State James Byrnes who were insistent on Japan's unconditional surrender. Under Secretary of State Joseph Grew was also against the dropping of the atomic bomb. Grew had experience working at the U.S. Embassy in Japan, and he was well versed on Japan's circumstances. He asserted the opinion that Japan would immediately surrender if that surrender was conditional upon the preservation of the imperial system. However, as President Truman and Secretary of State Byrnes had already given Japan notice of an unconditional surrender through the Potsdam Declaration, and it was thought that the peace faction on the Japan side, which had been insistent upon the preservation of the imperial system as a condition of surrender, would also reject the Potsdam Declaration.

After the war, it was reported in the media that Truman had been awarded an honorary degree from the University of Oxford, Britain. In response to this, British philosopher Elizabeth Anscombe strongly criticized the atomic bombing of Hiroshima and Nagasaki as a crime of killing innocent people. As stated above, while there are people who seek to justify the dropping of the atomic bomb, there are also many people, even in the Western countries, including the United States, who asserted opposition to the dropping of the atomic bomb.

Putting aside the question of whether the dropping of the atomic bomb was right or wrong, one must question whether there is justice and injustice among warring parties in the first place. Looking back on history, most conflicts arise out of assertions of justice against justice, and as a result, that is perhaps why so many conflicts end with it naturally being regarded that the victorious was just and the defeated was unjust. Just take the International Military Tribunal for the Far East as an example. At this tribunal, Japan, the defeated, were judged by the Allied Powers, the victors, for crimes against peace and crimes against humanity. It is certainly not possible to deny the fact that during the Second World War, Japan invaded other countries and committed atrocities. But then, in accepting this fact, is it enough to only judge the crimes committed by Japan, which is deemed to have carried out an unjust war? Are the crimes in war only applicable to the defeated? As mentioned previously, in this military tribunal, Judge Pal asserted that war crimes exist not only among the defeated but among the victors as well.

The United States, victor in the Japan-U.S. war, denounced Japan as follows: Japan entered the war without making a declaration by attacking Pearl Harbor; it committed inhumane treatment of prisoners of war; and it invaded countries such as China and killed numerous civilians. One wonders then how the victorious United States defends its actions in face of the following historical facts. Even if we assume for one moment that the dropping of the atomic bombs on Hiroshima and Nagasaki never occurred, did not the United States kill multitudes of civilians through indiscriminate air raids on cities pretty much throughout the entirety of Japan? Did it not use incendiary bombs in a massive aerial assault on Tokyo, burning to death about 100,000 civilians in a single night? While condemning the Nazi Holocaust, did it not participate in killing multitudes of German civilians through indiscriminate air raids on Dresden and Hamburg? How can the U.S. military assert that these were acts against humanity based on justice?

And what's more, was not the U.S. military's attack on Iraq in 2003 a start of war without a declaration? Were the weapons of mass destruction, which were used as the just cause for attacking Iraq, ever discovered? It is not only the Iraq War. What did the U.S. military do in Son My village? What did the Korean military do to civilians in Vietnamese villages? What did the Korean military do to its own citizens during the Korean War (Bodo League massacre)? What did the Pol Pot faction do to its own citizens in the Cambodian Civil War? What occurred in the Rwanda conflict in Africa? What did the Chinese Communist Party do to as many as tens of millions of citizens during the Cultural Revolution? What did the Soviet Union military do in the Katyn Forest in Poland during the Second World War? What did Stalin do to his own Soviet citizens in the name of repression?

Looking back further in history, the examples become endless. Did not the European and American powers colonize China, various East-Asian countries and India in the 19th century? Emigrants from Europe who became the ancestors of today's Americans snatched the land from the indigenous peoples, who had done no wrong, in the name of settlement of the American West in the North American Continent in

157

the 17th century. And what was done to them? Weren't many blacks brought from the African Continent as slaves and put to work like animals? What did Spain do to the Inca Empire in the 16th century? What did the crusaders do to the heathens in the name of God when they went on successive expeditions from the 11th century onward?

If we take an overseeing view of human history in this way, it consists of endlessly repeating atrocities that are called invasions and massacres, as we all know. How terrible these acts are. They are carried out on other humans as if the perpetrators' justice is the only justice, which is usually given the name of freedom or faith. I do not say these things so that I may justify my own country and denounce the inhumanity of other countries. Rather, I ask for renewed recollection of the constantly repeated inhumane acts that all peoples throughout the world inflict to a greater or lesser extent on other peoples.

Looking back on such human history from the past to the present, one wonders whether sometime in mankind's future we will arrive at an age where there are no wars. Certainly, the movement calling for no more Hiroshima and no more Nagasaki is spreading, and many organizations are advocating opposition to war and the disposal of nuclear weapons. However, on the other hand, the countries possessing nuclear weapons around the world continue to perform nuclear testing, and many countries are continuing to enhance their armaments. Some people pessimistically believe that wars will continue unless mankind learns to coexist, and I cannot easily dismiss such a view.

Among the creatures on this planet, humans have accomplished rapid evolution and prosperity. Somewhat paradoxically, however, our high intelligence is the reason we obtained the custom of killing each other. Although I look to the future of mankind with pessimism, I do not want to abandon any ray of hope. I think that not abandoning hope no matter the circumstances is an attribute that we Homo sapiens should hold onto with pride.

About seventy years have passed since my uncle left this world. My age has far exceeded my uncle's age when he died, and it has even reached a father's age. Even so, for me, my uncle will always reside in the spirit of a 15 year-old boy.

It is not possible for me to meet my uncle in this world. I find this a bitter truth. When I long to meet someone who is already dead, I think of the following words of philosopher Kiyoshi Miki. "If I had the chance to once again meet with them (the departed), it would make anything other than my own death impossible." "I know that I will never meet them again in this world. This probability is zero. Of course, I don't know for sure if I will meet them in death, but there is no one who knows for sure that this probability is zero. No one returns from the land of the dead to tell. When I compare the two probabilities, the latter may have a much larger possibility than the former. If I had to bet on it, I could not bet on anything other than the latter." ("Notes on Human Life" Miki Kiyoshi, 1938, Shinchosha Publishing)

These words stir my heart. If there were a possibility of meeting my uncle, then this way of thinking is the only way. If there were an afterworld, and I met a boy the age of a son to me, I probably would have to address him as uncle. I can't imagine such a scenario. While sentimental to the words of Kiyoshi Miki, I think that in all of eternity, I will never meet my uncle.

I sometimes imagine how it would have been if uncle was not killed by the atomic bomb and survived. While being totally engrossed in building model airplanes and going glider training from sun up to sun down, my uncle dreamed for the skies. Therefore, after graduating from school and joining society, he probably would have been employed in aircraft manufacturing. Then, while drinking sake together with me, we would have a pleasant talk that would probably make me laugh. And, we would probably together sing, "the evening rain, white on Carp Castle, matching the fading colors of the flowers in full bloom..." That song,

Evening of Carp Castle was known by any student of Hiroshima First Middle School, and it was also popular among the students when I was at senior high school.

I also wonder how post-war Japanese society would appear to my uncle. Although Japan had become a society at peace, I wonder if my uncle would say something like, "If this depraved world is peace time, we were better off before the war." Or perhaps because he didn't have any freedoms in his lifestyle during the war, he would say that he is happy there are now freedoms and affluence in life in Japan. Moreover, I wonder what his opinion would be about the atomic bomb being dropped on Hiroshima.

Again this year, various ceremonies are planned in the city of Hiroshima for the anniversary of the atomic bombing of Hiroshima on August 6. When the sun sets, I'm sure they will hold the annual floating of lanterns on the Motoyasu River that flows in front of the A-Bomb Dome. Thinking about this, I realize that at some point I stopped going to the annual floating lantern that I had gone to every year as a child. After growing up, I was overrun with study and work and I think I just stopped going. Perhaps also that strange tinge of sadness I always felt when I went to the floating lanterns as a child caused somewhere in my heart to hold me back. Whichever the case, nowadays, I once again feel like going to the place of the floating lanterns and honoring the memory of my uncle. The road in front of the A-Bomb Dome is the road that my uncle took as a junior high student when walking to and from school every day.

Afterword

My uncle was in third grade of Hiroshima Prefectural Hiroshima First Middle School (Hiroshima First Middle School) when the atomic bomb was dropped on Hiroshima on August 6, 1945. He was struck by the bomb while at school, about 900 meters from ground zero, and died on August 7, the next day. He died aged 15. This book is a compilation of the second half of my uncle's life.

On the day that the atomic bomb was dropped on Hiroshima, more than eight thousand junior high students were engaged in forced evacuation and demolition work inside the city. Of these students, about six thousand lost their lives.

The reason he was at school when the bomb struck was because he had attended school to perform air defense personnel duties. As Hiroshima First Middle School was located not far from ground zero, seven teachers, about 150 first graders, and a dozen or so third graders on duty as air defense personnel died within days of the explosion. Meanwhile, most of the third graders were away from school, either working in factories as part of labor mobilization, or engaged in the forced building evacuation and demolition. About 50 third graders who were engaged in the forced building evacuation and demolition around Dobashi close to ground zero died. However, among the rest of the third graders, there fortunately were no fatalities directly following the explosion, probably because they were further away from the blast.

As for my close family, a total of eight family members were bomb victims, including my parents, my uncles and grandfather on my father's side, and my grandparents and uncle on my mother's side. My parents died in their 70s and 80s and had lived healthy lives, never suffering the aftereffects of the bomb. All members of my family who were surviving bomb victims did not suffer any serious aftereffects caused by the atomic bomb. As second-generation bomb victims, I and my sister have lived our lives without any serious illness. My uncle was the only member of my family to have his life taken by the atomic bomb.

As I was born after the war, I never knew my uncle while he was alive. However, I have experienced an event that caused me to feel about my uncle as family. It occurred more than ten years ago. At this time, my father, my uncle's eldest brother, had already died and I was sorting through the mementos of my father. Among the mementos, mixed up with diaries my father had written while still a student, I found photos of my uncle, and letters written by my uncle, all carefully stored. It was good fortune that mementos of my uncle remained. Although the nuclear bomb had turned the family home to ashes, my grandfather had relocated precious items, and so photos of my uncle escaped from being burned. In addition, letters written by my uncle had been saved by relatives (they had fortunately escaped damage as my relatives lived outside of Hiroshima) and later returned to my father.

When I looked upon the photograph of my uncle for the first time, I was surprised how my uncle looked so much like I did at his age. Then I looked at the letters, which revealed that he was a playful, carefree teenager with a sense of humor; that he had become absorbed with model airplane making as an elementary school student; and that he had continued this passion into junior high school. When I thought that I too had become absorbed in model airplane making in my boyhood, and that my senior high school was the successor of Hiroshima First Middle School, I felt there was a mysterious connection between me and my uncle. It felt as if my uncle was telling me that he wanted me to leave some proof of his life.

That said, as I never knew my uncle when he was alive, it was a difficult task to depict the second half of his life. I decided to ask people who were in the same year at school as him to get some clues about him during his junior high school years. Fortunately for me, the senior high school that I graduated from shares the same alumni association as Hiroshima First Middle School. This allowed me to contact people who were in the same school year as my uncle. Thanks to this, people of the same school year who remembered my uncle provided me with valuable information. I was then able to conjure a concrete image of my uncle while he was at junior high. Among these contributions, I received valuable information and advice from, in no particular order, Messrs. Tadayuki Abe, Yorimi Sugo, Yoshio Kato, Kuniharu Sera, Susumu Zoriki, Shiro Nakayama, Heitaro Hamada, and Hiromu Morishita.

To be frank, it may not be possible for me to depict the terribleness of the atomic bomb as I was born after the war and did not experience the atomic bomb. Just as so many of the bomb victims say, I don't think anyone other than those who experienced it could possibly know the real horror of that day. Therefore, I cannot emphasize enough how big a help the assistance of the people of the same school year was. It would therefore be no overstatement to say that writing this book would have been impossible for me without the cooperation of these people. I received detailed help from Ms. Yoshiko Maehira of Gentosha Renaissance in bringing this book to published form, including intricate editing work from start to finish. I express my sincere gratitude to all these people.

Although it was my intention to provide an accurate account of the historic events mentioned in this book, when writing about the individual sphere, I invented some parts in my depictions. However, the invention that I used was not baseless fabrication but rather a depiction of what I thought most likely happened. This book mentions the locations of my uncle and his fellow third graders with respect to where the students of each class were located. However, as there were slight discrepancies in the testimonies of the people who were students of the same year, more investigation would have been required to ensure the accuracy of the information. The time at which the atomic bomb exploded is stated in this book not 8:15 a.m. but 8:16 a.m. The American resources state it was 8:16 a.m. and this book follows the references that are cited.

The content of this book is simply a personal record that compiles the second half of the life of my uncle. Even so, if readers of this book developed a greater understanding of the atrocity of war and the menace of nuclear weapons, and felt that such tragedies must not be repeated, I would like to think that my uncle would be satisfied by such a result.

Bibliography

Ogura, Toyofumi. *Zetsugo no Kiroku Naki Tsuma he no Tegami.* Chuosha 1948 (In Japanese.) (Translation available: Ogura, Toyofumi. Trans. Murakami, Kisaburo; Fujii, Shigeru. *Letters from the End of the World: A Firsthand Account of the Bombing of Hiroshima*)

Ed. Akita, Masayuki. *Hoshi wa Miteiru.* Masushobo (now Intelfin Inc.) 1954. (In Japanese.)

Ed. Hiroshima City. *Hiroshima Genbaku Sensaishi* (Record of the Hiroshima A-bomb War Disaster) Volume 1–5 Hiroshima City. 1970. (In Japanese.)

Ed. Hiroshima Prefectural Hiroshima First Middle School Bomb Victim Students Association. *Yukari no Tomo.* Hiroshima Prefectural Hiroshima First Middle School Bomb Victim Students Association. 1965. (In Japanese.)

Ed. Hiroshima City Genbaku Taikenkikai. *Genbaku Taikenki* (A Record of A-bomb Experiences) Asahi Shimbun Publishing Co. 1975. (In Japanese.)

Ed. Hiroshima Prefectural Hiroshima Kokutaiji High School Centenary Journal. *Hiroshima First Middle School Kokutaiji Centenary.* Mother School Foundation Centenary Project. 1977. (In Japanese.)

Ed. Hiroshima City & Nagasaki City Journal of A-Bomb Disaster. *Hiroshima Nagasaki A-Bomb Disaster.* Iwanami Shoten. 1975. (In Japanese.)

Thomas, Gordon; Morgan-Witts, Max. Trans. Matsuda, Sen. *Enola Gay —Mission to Hiroshima*. TBS Britannica. 1980.

Kouchi, Akira. *Hiroshima no Sora ni Hiraita Rakkasan* (Parachutes in Hiroshima's Sky). Daiwa Shobo. 1985. (In Japanese.)

Thomas, Gordon; Morgan-Witts, Max. *Enola Gay—Mission to Hiroshima*. White Owl Press. 1995.

Takaki, Ronald. *Hiroshima: Why America Dropped the Atomic Bomb*. Little, Brown and Company. 1995.

Takaki, Ronald. Trans. Yamaoka, Yoichi. *Hiroshima: Why America Dropped the Atomic Bomb*. Soshisha. 1995. (In Japanese.)

Nakayama, Shiro. *Watashi no Hiroshima Chizu* (My Hiroshima Map). Nishidashoten. 1998.

Walker, Stephen. Trans. Yokoyama, Hiroaki. *Countdown to Hiroshima*. Hayakawa Publishing Corporation. 2005.

Pal, Rabhabinod and Tanaka, Masaaki. *Judge Pal's 'Peace Declaration'* Shogakukan 2008. (In Japanese.)

Miscamble, Wilson D. The Most Controversial Decision: *Truman, the Atomic Bombs, and the Defeat of Japan*. Cambridge University Press, 2011.

Hamada, Heitaro. *Izumi Genbaku to Watashi* (Spring — The A-Bomb and I) Vol. 2. 2012.

About the Author:

Toshinori Kanaya was born in Hiroshima city, 1951. He graduated from Hiroshima Kokutaiji High and Hiroshima University Faculty of Medicine where he obtained a Doctor of Medicine. After working in hospitals, he opened a medical practice in northern Hiroshima Prefecture in 1993.

His other books in Japanese include Okitsune Kikkawa (about a military commander in 16th century Hiroshima), Buichi Uprising (about an agrarian revolt in 19th century Hiroshima), and Mouri Takamoto (about a military commander in 16th century Hiroshima). All were published by Chuokoron Jigyo Shuppan.

email: toshinori.kanaya.hiroshima@gmail.com

Notes

Made in the USA
Las Vegas, NV
17 January 2024

84404554R00100